'I'm so sorry, Libby,' he whispered. 'So very, very sorry for letting you down.'

'Seb, have you got a minute?'

He looked round when the door suddenly opened and Cathy appeared. 'Problems?' he said, standing up. Libby hadn't moved; she was still curled up asleep. He doubted if she was aware that he was there, which probably wasn't a bad thing. He was feeling far too emotional at the moment, and he couldn't afford to feel this way if he hoped to convince her that their marriage could work if she'd only give him a second chance.

He had to be focussed, centred, he thought as he followed Cathy out of the door. He had to present the idea of them trying again to her with confidence and assurance, so that she would believe it was worth taking the risk. He knew it was a lot to ask, and that he didn't deserve another chance after the mess he'd made of things, but he couldn't just let her go without a struggle. He needed her, wanted her, loved her, and by heaven he was going to tell her that before this night was over. He wanted his wife back for keeps!

A&E DRAMA

Blood pressure is high and pulses are racing
in these fast-paced dramatic stories from
Mills & Boon® Medical Romance™.
They'll move a mountain to save a life
in an emergency, be they the crash team,
emergency doctors, or paramedics.
There are lots of critical engagements
amongst the high tensions and emotional
passions in these exciting stories of
lives and loves at risk!

A NIGHT
TO REMEMBER

BY
JENNIFER TAYLOR

MILLS & BOON®

First published in Great Britain 2006
Large Print edition 2007
Harlequin Mills & Boon Limited,
Eton House, 18-24 Paradise Road,
Richmond, Surrey TW9 1SR

© Jennifer Taylor 2006

ISBN-13: 978 0 263 19344 2
ISBN-10:   0 263 19344 6

Set in Times Roman 17 on 19¾ pt.
17-0407-49873

Printed and bound in Great Britain
by Antony Rowe Ltd, Chippenham, Wiltshire

Dear Reader

We read so much in the press about the number of marriages which fail that it's easy to forget about those which survive. I wrote this book in the hope that it would redress the balance a little.

When Libby Bridges sets out to tell her husband, Seb, that she wants a divorce, she is sure that she is doing the right thing. They have drifted so far apart that their marriage is little more than a sham. However, during the course of the following twenty-four hours, as she and Seb are forced to work together, Libby finds herself reassessing her decision. Does she really want to lose Seb?

Seb is devastated when he realises why Libby has come to see him. He desperately wants to persuade her to give him a second chance, but as the night passes, and one crisis succeeds another, time is slipping away. Will he be able to convince Libby that he still needs her?

I had great fun writing this book to a time scale. As each hour passes, bringing the time when Libby and Seb must part ever closer, I found myself willing them to admit the truth—that they love one another and want to stay together. Did they manage it in the end? You will have to read the book to find out!

Best wishes

Jennifer

Jennifer Taylor lives in the north-west of England with her husband Bill. She had been writing Mills & Boon® romances for some years, but when she discovered Medical Romances™, she was so captivated by these heart-warming stories that she set out to write them herself! When she's not writing, or doing research for her latest book, Jennifer's hobbies include reading, travel, walking her dog and retail therapy (shopping!). Jennifer claims all that bending and stretching to reach the shelves is the best exercise possible. She's always delighted to hear from readers, so do visit her at www.jennifer-taylor.com

Recent titles by the same author:

A BABY OF HIS OWN†
THE CONSULTANT'S ADOPTED SON†
IN HIS LOVING CARE†
NURSE IN A MILLION*
THE FOREVER ASSIGNMENT*
A SPECIAL KIND OF CARING

*Worlds Together
†Bachelor Dads

CHAPTER ONE

Friday: 3 p.m.

THE sky had that leaden look that usually heralded a storm. Libby Bridges pulled into a lay-by and checked her map. If there was a storm brewing, she wanted to get to her destination as quickly as possible.

Her finger traced the network of roads and she sighed. By her reckoning, she still had another fifty miles to go before she reached the hospital. Maybe she should phone Seb and warn him that she was coming so he would wait for her. She didn't want him to leave work before she got there. Although he had sent her his new address when he had moved, she had never been to the house and wasn't sure if she would be able to find it on her own.

Libby took her mobile phone out of her bag but even as she went to key in the number, she changed her mind. If she phoned Seb and told him that she was on her way to see him, he would want to know why. Did she really intend to tell him over the phone that she wanted a divorce? Maybe they hadn't been able to make their marriage work but the least she could do was to end it with dignity.

She shoved the phone back into her bag and pulled out onto the road, but her heart was heavy as she set off again. She wasn't looking forward to the next few hours but what choice did she have? There was no point hoping that she and Seb could work things out because they had passed that point now. The problem was that they were two very different people to the starry-eyed lovers who had met at med school and married on the day they had graduated.

Just remembering all the dreams they'd had once for their future together was almost too painful. They had been so sure that their love would last but the strain of working increasingly long hours had taken its toll. Whole weeks had passed when they had barely seen each other if one of them had been working nights. That was the main reason why she had decided to go into general practice. Working set hours—even long ones—had seemed preferable to never seeing Seb and it had been fine at first, until he'd been offered his dream job in the north-east.

Libby's pretty mouth compressed as she remembered the argument they'd had when Seb had told her that he was considering taking up the post. She was just getting settled into the practice in Sussex and starting to find her feet when he had dropped his bombshell. They'd ended up having a massive row. She'd told him that he was selfish for expecting her to give up her job and follow him around the country, and he had accused her of having a closed mind. They had gone round and round in circles, neither of them willing to give an inch, until in the end they had gone to bed with the problem still unresolved.

She sighed. That was the first time they'd

slept in separate beds since their marriage and it had been their biggest mistake of all. Each time they'd had an argument after that, one of them had retired to the spare room. They had never actually sat down and tried to talk through their problems. They had shut themselves away and, inevitably, they had grown apart.

When Seb had taken up the post as consultant in charge of the newly opened trauma unit on the north-east coast, they had made an effort at first: Seb had driven down to Sussex one weekend and she had driven up the next. However, they had both known that they wouldn't be able to keep up such a gruelling routine. Something had had to give and in the end it had been their marriage. Now it was time to take the final step and end it. At least this way they might have some good memories to look back on.

'Clear!'

Seb Bridges placed the paddles on the boy's chest and sent another surge of electricity arcing through the nine-year-old's body. Young Liam Baxter had had a fight with a bus on his way home from school and he had come off worst.

'Come on, come on,' Seb muttered, his dark brows drawn into a frown as he willed the child's heart to start beating again.

'Sinus rhythm,' the nurse beside him announced, and a collective cheer went up. Seb grinned at his team.

'Well done, you lot. That's another one we can chalk up as a success. Carry on like this and we'll start winning awards!'

Everyone laughed at that. The idea of them being afforded any credit for their efforts was a pipe dream. With government targets to meet, not to mention patients' increasingly high expectations, they were lucky if they received the odd thank you most days. Cathy, the senior charge nurse on the trauma unit, rolled her eyes at him.

'You still haven't got rid of those high-faluting southern expectations, have you, Seb?'

'Are you calling me a dreamer, hen?' he demanded in his best imitation of the local accent.

'If the cap fits…'

Cathy stuck her nose in the air and whisked past him. Seb laughed. One of the best things about this job was the camaraderie he enjoyed with his team. They were a great bunch, every single one of them as dedicated as he was. He really had struck lucky when he'd made the move north. Not only had he found his dream job but he'd made a lot of good friends, too. It had helped make up in a small way for all that he'd lost.

A familiar pain stabbed his heart at the thought of Libby and he swung round so his colleagues wouldn't see his anguish. There were patients waiting to be seen, and there was no time to waste by thinking about the mess he had made of his marriage. All the regrets in the world wouldn't change things now.

He left Resus and went to check the white-board. Every single cubicle was occupied and there was a patient in the treatment room as well. It had been an exceptionally busy day, even by their standards. The closure of several smaller accident and emergency units in the surrounding area had put extra pressure on them. The Grace Darling Hospital's trauma unit was not only a centre of excellence, it was the main provider of emergency care for several hundred thousand people. Now he glanced round when his junior registrar, Gary Parr, came hurrying over to him.

'Looks like your average day in the madhouse,' he observed drolly.

'And it's about to get worse, by all accounts.' Gary looked worried as he drew Seb aside. 'We've just had the coastguard on the phone. Apparently, there's a tanker adrift in the North Sea and it's on course to hit one of the off-shore gas platforms.'

'Hell! What's the tanker carrying?' Seb demanded.

'Some sort of chemicals, although they're not sure exactly what yet. The coastguard is still trying to get the information out of the tanker's owners and they aren't being very co-operative, it seems.'

'Does the coastguard think they might be able to head it off?' Seb asked, frowning as he considered the implications of such a scenario.

Obviously there would be casualties from both the tanker and the drilling rig if there was a collision, but that wasn't his only concern. If there was a chemical spillage, it could spread for miles along the coastline and that would put many more people at risk.

'There are tugs on their way to it but it doesn't sound very hopeful.' Gary grimaced. 'The coastguard says there's a storm brewing and it's going to be a bad one, too. The guy I spoke to didn't rate their chances of avoiding a collision very highly.'

'In that case, we need to prepare for the worst-case scenario.' Seb swung round and headed for the office. Gary followed him inside and closed the door.

'You think it warrants major incident status?' the younger doctor asked, going pale at the thought.

'I think it's worth putting everyone on standby,' Seb told him firmly, picking up the phone. 'The last thing we need is to be caught flat-footed.'

He dialled the major incident headquarters

and asked to speak to the duty officer. He was put straight through, although he didn't need to explain why he was phoning—the coastguard had beaten him to it. He nodded when the duty officer explained that an announcement was being prepared and that it would be aired over local radio within the next half-hour.

He hung up and opened the top drawer of the filing cabinet. He took out the file that contained the names of all the staff who were designated to work during a major incident and handed it to Gary.

'Check who's already here then make a list of the others so the switchboard can contact them, will you? I'll go and tell everyone what's happened and start winding things down in here. The last thing we need is a waiting room full of patients if we end up with a major emergency on our hands.'

'What about the air ambulance service?' Gary asked hurriedly as Seb made for the door. 'Do I need to get in touch with them, too?'

'You may as well, although they probably know about it by now.' Seb turned and stared out of the window, sighing when he saw the black clouds that were massing overhead. 'It looks as though it's going to be a very long night.'

CHAPTER TWO

Friday: 4 p.m.

THE storm broke just as Libby was turning in through the gates of the hospital. Raindrops as big as golf balls struck the windscreen, forcing her to slow down to a crawl. She switched on the wipers to their fastest setting but even then they couldn't cope with the deluge.

Rubbing the back of her hand over the glass to clear away the condensation that was forming on it, she peered out. There was a sign up ahead, directing her to the car park, so she cautiously headed in that direction, surprised by the size of the hospital complex. Seb had told her that a whole new wing had been built to house the trauma unit during the recent renovations but she'd not realised before just how impressive it was.

No wonder he'd wanted to work here, she thought as she searched for a parking place. He had always enjoyed being in the thick of things and thrived in a crowd, whereas she preferred to be with a small group of people whom she knew well. She frowned as she manoeuvred the car into an empty space. She'd never realised before how different they were in that respect.

She switched off the engine then found her umbrella. Opening the car door, she stepped out and gasped when the wind immediately tore the umbrella from her hand as soon as she tried to open it. It went bouncing across the car park, its spokes getting battered and broken as it was tumbled around. She sighed as she locked the car doors. There was no point going after it so she would just have to get soaked, although it was annoying when she'd wanted to appear totally in control when she saw Seb.

She made her way from the car park and followed the signs directing her to the trauma unit. Even though it was barely four o'clock, the light was fading fast. The storm was gathering momentum and she was relieved when she spotted the entrance up ahead. If the wind got any stronger, she doubted if she'd be able to stay on her feet and that would be the last straw—to turn up at Seb's place of work covered in mud!

Libby hurried inside the building then paused to get her bearings. The reception desk was straight ahead with a large waiting area to the right. Rows of chairs were neatly lined up in there and there was a drinks machine in the corner next to a rack of magazines. The place looked exactly as she had expected it would do, apart from one major omission: there were no people.

Where were all the patients? she wondered, looking around. The walking wounded as well as the seriously injured who filled up every accident and emergency department in the country? She couldn't believe this was a normal Friday afternoon. Seb had told her several times how busy he was and that there weren't enough hours in the day to see all the people who turned up. Obviously, something must have happened…

'I'm afraid the emergency department is closed at the moment.'

Libby swung round when a nurse suddenly appeared. 'I'm not a patient,' she explained hurriedly. 'I'm here to see Dr Bridges.'

'Dr Bridges is too busy to see anyone at the moment,' the nurse said firmly. 'I'm sorry, but I'm going to have to ask you to leave.'

'Libby!'

They both turned when they heard Seb's voice. Libby summoned a smile but she could see the shock on his face as he moved towards her. 'Hello, Seb. I seem to have chosen a bad time to arrive. Sorry.'

'There's no need to apologise. You weren't to know that we were in the middle of a major incident alert.'

He returned her smile but she could hear the tension in his deep voice. Was he wondering why she had turned up like this, out of the blue? It was three months since they'd seen each other, and that meeting couldn't be classed as a success by any stretch of the imagination. The weekend had been a strain for both of them; they'd found it difficult to think of anything to say most of the time. They had drifted so far apart now that they seemed to have no common ground any more.

She'd been relieved when Seb had decided to cut short his visit and return to the north-east. However, it had been that meeting which had helped her make up her mind about what she wanted to do. It had proved once and for all that their marriage was dead and that the best thing would be to end it rather than allow it to drag on.

Now here she was, about to do that very thing, yet she couldn't just baldly announce her decision. She and Seb needed to sit down and work out the details, like who should have which items of furniture, for instance. However, the likelihood of them being able to do that now seemed extremely remote.

'Sorry. I'm forgetting my manners. I should have introduced you two. Cathy, I'd like you to meet my wife, Libby. Or Dr Olivia Bridges, if you'd prefer her official title.'

Libby summoned a smile as Seb introduced her to the other woman but she could see the wariness in his eyes when he turned to her and knew that she was right. He had guessed why she'd come and she wasn't sure if that made the situation better or worse.

'Libby, this is Cathy Watts, the senior charge nurse on the unit. This place would grind to a halt without her!'

'It's good to meet you, Cathy,' she said quietly, offering the other woman her hand.

'You too, Dr Bridges.'

The nurse shook her hand but Libby detected a definite coolness about her manner, which surprised her. Although Cathy had gone through the motions, she didn't appear to be exactly enthusiastic about meeting her and, frankly, Libby couldn't understand why... Unless Cathy had more than a professional interest in Seb, in which case she would hardly be thrilled to see her there, would she?

The thought that Seb might be seeing another woman was one that had crossed her mind several times in the past year, although she had always dismissed it before. He had never done or said anything to suggest that he was having an affair so she had given him the benefit of the doubt. However, she realised all of a sudden it would be naïve to imagine that a man like Seb would be on his own for very long.

Her gaze skimmed up the long, powerful lines of his body and she felt a little shiver run through her. He'd always had a huge physical impact on her from the first moment they'd met. Tall and dark with the kind of leanly hewn good looks that appealed to so many women, Seb had been her first and her only lover. That he'd had other relationships before he'd met her had never bothered her. It had been enough to know that she had been the one he'd wanted and chosen to marry.

Now everything had changed and it was too much to expect that a man as attractive and virile as her husband would have been content to live the life of a monk these past months. Had he been seeing Cathy, or someone else? Maybe it wasn't her business any more, but she was only human. She couldn't help wanting to know the answer.

Seb could feel the shock waves spreading through his entire body. Seeing Libby standing there had knocked him for six. He'd physically had to restrain himself when what he'd wanted to do had been to sweep her into his arms and kiss her until every doubt that had plagued him since their last meeting had been erased for good. It was only the thought of why she'd driven all the way up here to see him that had stopped him. Had she come to ask him for a divorce? He didn't want to believe it—hell, he couldn't bear to believe it!—yet he knew in his heart it was true. As far as Libby was concerned, their marriage was over.

Pain sliced through him, but before he could say anything to her the main doors burst open and a man ran into the unit.

'It's my wife… She's outside in the car… Please, you have to help her!'

'I'll be right there.' Seb hurriedly set aside his own feelings as he turned to Cathy. 'Find

Marilyn and tell her that I need her in Resus, stat. I'll take the patient straight there so you and Jayne get everything ready.'

'Will do,' the nurse assured him.

Seb didn't waste any time as he hurried outside. There was a car parked all askew in front of the door and he could see a young woman lying on the back seat. 'What happened to her?' he asked as the driver opened the car door.

'I don't know!' The driver was frantic with worry as he climbed into the car and attempted to lift his wife out. She screamed in agony when he moved her and Seb quickly put a restraining hand on his arm.

'Let me take a look at her first.' He waited while the man scrambled back out of the car then bent down to speak to the young woman. Her eyes were glazed with pain and she was clutching her stomach.

'My name is Seb Bridges and I'm the consultant in charge of the trauma unit. Can you tell me when this all started?'

'I'm not sure… An hour ago…maybe more…' She broke off and groaned. 'It hurts!'

Seb glanced round, intending to tell her husband to go back inside and ask one of the porters to fetch out a trolley. He did a double-take when he discovered that Libby had followed him outside and was standing behind him.

'Do you need a trolley?' she asked, anticipating his request.

'Please.' He swiftly battened down his emotions. It really wasn't the right moment to think about all the other times when she had seemingly read his mind. 'Get one of the porters to bring it out here. I'll need him to help me move her. There's no way she can walk in this state.'

'Of course.'

She hurried away as he crouched down beside the car again. He gently eased the woman's hands away from her abdomen, but she cried out in pain when he tried to examine her and he paused.

'I know it hurts but I need to find out what's going on in there. Just yell if the pain gets too much for you. I have very strong nerves so don't worry about scaring me.'

She seemed reassured by his tone and allowed him to continue, moaning softly as he carried out a rudimentary examination. The abdominal wall was rock hard to his touch, the underlying muscles obviously in spasm. The pain seemed to be worse in the lower abdomen; the patient certainly complained loudest when he probed that area. However, before he could ask her any questions which might have helped with his diagnosis, Libby arrived with a porter and the trolley he'd requested.

Seb backed out of the car and turned to the patient's husband. 'We need to get your wife onto that trolley but it's not going to be easy for her. She's in a great deal of pain and it will hurt her even more when we try to move her.'

The young man blanched. 'I've never heard Alison cry like that before. She's quite tough, really, and never makes a fuss.'

'Which just proves how uncomfortable she is at the moment,' Libby said gently, stepping forward.

She laid her hand on the young man's arm and Seb felt a little flicker of resentment run through him when he saw her smile warmly at him. It had been a long time since she'd smiled at *him* that way, he thought before he realised how churlishly he was behaving.

'Make sure she knows you're here for her,' Libby continued, blissfully unaware of any undercurrents. 'Talk to her while we move her and hold her hand…anything that might help to reassure her. She's in pain and she's scared and she needs you to be strong for her.'

'I'll try.'

The young man seemed far more resolute as he bent down and spoke to his wife. The fact that he was no longer so panic-stricken obviously had an effect on her, too, because she immediately started to calm down. Seb told the porter to go round to the other side of the car so they could begin the process of lifting her out, but he couldn't help thinking how typical it was that Libby had managed to calm the situation down so effectively.

She'd always been good at finding the right words to reassure people. He had learned a lot from her when they had worked together, in fact. He'd had a tendency to rush because he'd wanted to get the job done, but she had taught him to be patient and spend an extra few minutes settling a patient down.

It had been the same in their private life: Libby had been the calm one, the one who had kept things ticking over, whereas he'd always been rushing around, trying to do ten jobs at once. He had always believed that they complemented each other in that respect, that her calmness was the perfect foil for his impatience. But was that really true? Or was it more a case of them being complete opposites who approached life from different directions and had very little in common?

His heart sank because it seemed the more likely explanation. He and Libby didn't complement each other—they opposed one another. Was it any wonder in those circumstances that she had given up on their marriage?

CHAPTER THREE

Friday: 5 p.m.

'THANK you, Dr Bridges. I'll take over from here.'

Libby moved aside as Cathy Watts came hurrying over and took her place beside the trolley. It was obvious that the charge nurse expected her to leave Resus, but for some reason she felt loath to do so. She glanced at Seb, who was standing by the bed, and sighed. Surely she wasn't jealous at the thought of the other woman being there to assist him while she'd been dismissed as surplus to requirements?

'On my count, everyone,' Seb said. 'One… two…three.'

The young woman was swiftly transferred onto the bed and the team sprang into action.

It was obviously a well-rehearsed routine because nobody needed to be told what to do. While Seb was delicately probing the patient's abdomen, Cathy was attaching her to various monitor leads. Another nurse—Jayne, according to her name badge—had begun to remove the woman's clothing, and the specialist registrar, Marilyn Maddocks, was taking a blood sample.

Libby had to admit that she was impressed by the ease with which they slotted into their allotted roles, although she wasn't surprised. Seb had always demanded the very highest standards from his staff because it was what he demanded from himself.

'Do you have any pain anywhere else, Alison?'

Seb's voice was clear and deep as he asked the patient various questions, and Libby shivered. She had always loved the sound of his voice. It had been the first thing that had attracted her to him, in fact. She'd been in the students' union at the time, attempting to buy herself a glass of wine and failing miserably. The place had been packed that night and making herself heard above the din had been a major task. But then Seb had appeared and asked her what she'd wanted and, lo and behold, a glass had materialised in front of her as though by magic.

He had picked it up and led her over to a table—typically, he'd been able to find an empty one even in that crush—and then he had proceeded to charm her. By the end of the night she'd been more than halfway in love with him and by the end of the month they had moved in together. They had lived together all through med school and even though she had found the course extremely hard going at times, she had got through it because Seb had been there to help and encourage her.

She sighed. At one time she'd believed that he would always be there for her but it hadn't worked out that way. Now she had accepted that divorce was the only answer. Once they made their separation legal, they would be free to get on with their lives, although she wasn't foolish enough to think that it would be easy for either of them. Their relationship had been very special and there were bound to be regrets on both sides. However, painful though it might be, she knew they couldn't carry on living the way they'd been doing for the past year. No, it would be better to end their marriage than endure any more heartache.

Seb frowned as he listened to what the patient was saying. 'So where exactly was this other pain, then?'

'In my shoulder…just here…' Alison's hand fluttered weakly as she touched the tip of her right shoulder, and he nodded.

'I see,' he said quietly, not wanting her to know how significant that snippet of information might turn out to be. He glanced over at Libby, wondering if she was adding up the clues as he was doing, and felt his heart jolt painfully when he saw the sadness on her face. She looked so unhappy that he longed to comfort her, but how could he when he had a patient who needed his help?

'Have you experienced any vaginal bleeding?'

he continued, doing his best to appear calmly in control, although his insides felt as though they were on a merry-go-round. Even if he lived to be a hundred, he doubted if he would ever fully recover from the shock of seeing Libby standing in the waiting room.

'I'm having a period at the moment,' Alison muttered, obviously embarrassed at having to talk about something so personal.

'So there's no possibility that you might be pregnant?' he persisted. 'You haven't missed a period recently?'

'Well, I didn't have one last month, but I'd just stopped taking the Pill and my GP warned me that my periods could be a bit erratic at first,' Alison explained, blushing furiously.

'Did you do a home pregnancy test?' Seb asked, checking the monitor readings. Although Alison's pulse, BP and heart rate were still within acceptable limits, there had been a slight deterioration in her condition so he decided not to waste any more time.

'Tell Ben I'm going to need a transvaginal ultrasound done, will you?' he told Cathy quietly, then turned back to the young woman as she answered his question.

'No, I didn't do a test. I didn't think there was any need to do one because of what my GP had said.' Alison was starting to look really scared now. 'Do you think I'm having a miscarriage, Doctor?'

'It's possibly a little more complicated than that,' Seb said gently. He nodded when Marilyn murmured that she would get onto the obstetric's registrar. Obviously, she'd latched onto his train of thought so he could save his explanations for the patient. Moving to the head of the bed again, he did all he could to sound reassuring but he could tell how terrified the young woman was.

'It's possible that you've had an ectopic pregnancy, Alison. What that means is that instead of the embryo developing inside your womb, it started to develop somewhere else. The most common place is in one of the Fallopian tubes but we'll have a better idea after you've had an ultrasound scan.'

'But what's going to happen if the baby's

growing in the wrong place? Will you be able to put it back where it's supposed to be?'

'No. I'm really sorry but that simply isn't possible.' Seb squeezed her hand when he saw tears ooze from her eyes. 'It's more than likely that the embryo is dead so it will be removed, along with any other damaged tissue.'

'And that's all that will happen?' the girl said through her sobs.

'A lot will depend on how much damage has been done. If the embryo has developed in one of your Fallopian tubes, the tube might have ruptured and the surgeon will have to decide if he can repair it.' He squeezed her hand tighter. 'If that isn't possible then the tube will need to be removed as well.'

'Oh!'

The girl broke into a storm of weeping. Seb sighed, wishing that he knew of a way to make this easier for her. He looked up when Libby suddenly appeared at his side.

'Let me talk to her,' she said simply.

Seb stepped aside, only half listening as Cathy came over to tell him that Ben was ready to do the scan. Libby was bending over the girl, stroking her hair and murmuring to her. Although Alison was still crying, whatever Libby was saying to her was obviously helping.

If only she would turn her talents to making their marriage better, he thought wistfully, then swung round because there was no point torturing himself with 'if onlys'. What was done was done and he had to live with the consequences, even though he had no idea how he was going to do that. How did you manage to live without the person you loved most in the whole world?

Libby sighed sadly as she watched Alison being whisked away. Once an ectopic pregnancy was confirmed, the girl would be taken to the obs and gynae unit and prepared for surgery. She felt very sorry for her. It must be a terrible shock for a woman to discover that she was pregnant and that there was no hope of her baby surviving.

'Thanks for that. I really appreciated it.'

She summoned a smile when Seb came over to her. 'It was the least I could do.'

'I'm still grateful, though. You've always had the gift of soothing people when they're at their lowest ebb.' He shrugged when she looked at him in surprise. 'Not many folk have that talent, Libby, but you do.'

'I…um…well, thank you.' She stumbled over the words and had to make an effort to collect herself, but it was odd that Seb should have said that after what she'd been thinking about him. 'We had a case similar to this during our first rotation on Casualty, if you remember,' she said quickly, not wanting to go back down that route again.

'Oh, I remember all right.' He rolled his eyes. 'A woman came in complaining of pains in her abdomen so we ran through everything we could think of—appendicitis, food poisoning, cystitis…'

'Abdominal colic.' She laughed. 'We hadn't a clue, had we?'

'No, we hadn't. We'd still be struggling if the senior reg hadn't come along and demanded to know if she had a pain in her shoulder.' Seb grinned. 'We thought he'd completely lost the plot by asking a question like that, until he informed us that shoulder-tip pain is often a symptom of an ectopic pregnancy.'

'We'd never even heard of it until then,' Libby agreed. 'He had to explain that it was caused by internal bleeding irritating the diaphragm when the patient breathes in and out.'

'It was one lesson we never forgot, though, especially as we got a real rollicking from him afterwards. What did he call us?'

'A pair of half-baked, incompetent morons who shouldn't be allowed anywhere near a member of the public,' she supplied helpfully, and he laughed.

'That's exactly what he said! How on earth did you remember after all this time?'

'Because that day stuck in my mind for a number of reasons.'

As soon as the words left her mouth Libby wished she hadn't said them, but it was too late by then. She could tell that Seb had remembered what else had happened that day, too.

After their roasting, they had gone back to their flat and one thing had led to another. They'd ended up making love and afterwards, as they had lain in one another's arms, Seb had asked her to marry him…

'Right. I'd better go and brief the team so that everyone knows what to expect,' he said brusquely, swinging round.

'You mean about this major incident? What's happened exactly?' She shrugged when he paused, not wanting him to know how painful it was to recall happier times. There was no point looking back but it wasn't easy to block out the memories when they were together. 'I never got a chance to ask you before because we were interrupted. It must be pretty serious, though, if you've closed the whole unit.'

'It is. There's a tanker adrift and it's on course to collide with one of the off-shore drilling rigs. We'll be treating the bulk of the casualties so it's going to get rather hectic around here.'

'Good heavens! It really is a major incident.'

'It's certainly the biggest thing we've had to

deal with since the unit opened.' He glanced at his watch and sighed. 'I'm sorry but I really need to get everything sorted out.'

'Of course you do. Sorry. I didn't mean to hold you up.'

'You haven't.' There was a moment when she thought he was going to say something else but in the end he merely shrugged. 'Why don't you come with me? That way I can introduce you to the rest of the team before it gets too busy.'

'Are you sure? I wouldn't want to get in the way.'

'You won't,' he said firmly, opening the door.

Libby wasn't convinced but it would have wasted too much time if she'd argued the point with him. She sighed as she followed him out of Resus. It certainly hadn't been the best time to turn up here. Seb had enough to contend with at the moment without her adding to the pressure. She just had to hold onto the thought that she was doing the right thing. For both of them.

CHAPTER FOUR

Friday: 6 p.m.

'SORRY to keep you waiting, but we had a bit of an emergency.'

Seb could feel his stomach churning as he led the way into the office. He beckoned Libby forward and dredged up a smile. 'For those of you who haven't met her yet, this is my wife, Libby. I'm afraid we'll have to leave the rest of the introductions until later, though.'

He closed the door, ignoring the looks that were being exchanged. Although everyone knew he was married, he guessed that most people had assumed that he and Libby were separated. It must be almost as big a shock for them as it had been for him to have her turn up like this, but there was nothing he could do about it. He could hardly explain why she'd come when he didn't *officially* know the reason himself.

'Right, I've spoken to the coastguard and the news isn't good,' he said briskly, trying not to dwell on how he was going to feel when Libby asked him for a divorce. 'The tugs have been unable to get a line to the tanker because of the heavy seas. It's still on course for a collision so they've decided to evacuate as many people as possible from the rig.'

'By helicopter?' Marilyn put in.

'To begin with. However, if the wind speed increases then the helicopters won't be able to continue flying so they've put out a call to all shipping in the area. If the local fishing boats can offload some of the crew, that will cut down the number of flights the air-sea rescue guys will have to make.' He shrugged. 'We don't want to add to the chaos by having a 'copter ditch in the sea.'

'How many crew are there on the tanker?' Ben Robertson, their senior radiologist, enquired.

'That's something the coastguard is still trying to establish, along with the exact nature of the cargo the tanker is carrying. Let's just say that the owners of the vessel are a tad reluctant to answer any questions.'

'So we don't know how many potential casualties we could end up with,' Cathy said in dismay.

'That's the top and bottom of it, I'm afraid.' Seb glanced around the room, his eyes lingering only a fraction longer on Libby than they did on anyone else but even so, he could have recited from memory every detail of what she was wearing if he'd been asked to do so.

He'd always loved her in blue, he thought wistfully. It was a colour that suited her perfectly, highlighting her honey-gold hair and fair skin. She'd worn a pale blue suit when they had married in the simple register office ceremony they had decided on. Neither of them had wanted a big wedding with lots of fuss. They'd just wanted each other and the day had been perfect. They had made their vows in front of a handful of family and friends, and they had both cried. It had been the best day of his life and it was almost too painful to have to remember it now.

He cleared his throat, afraid that his feelings would be all too apparent. 'We don't know if we'll be dealing with six or sixty casualties so we need to be prepared for every eventuality. Ambulance Control has been instructed to send only the most severely injured patients to us during the course of the next twenty-four hours so that should help, but if the numbers are high, we are going to be pushed to our absolute limit. Just do your best. That's all any of us can do.'

There was a murmur of agreement before everyone started to leave. Seb didn't go with them. They knew the drill and he didn't need to check up on what they were doing. Every single member of the team would do his or her job without him having to badger them. It was what made them work so well together: they trusted each other and had the kind of confidence that came from knowing they were trusted, too.

His gaze went to Libby again and his heart

ached with a searing pain. Libby had also trusted him at one time. She'd trusted him to be there for her and he had let her down. Maybe it had been his dream to work in a job like this, but could he put his hand on his heart and swear that it had been worth doing it when it had added to the demise of his marriage?

He wished he could, wished with every fibre of his being that he could say that his job had made up for what he'd lost, but he couldn't. He may have fulfilled his ambitions but he had lost Libby, and nothing could ever make up for that.

'I really think I should leave.'

Libby edged towards the door. It was obvious that Seb didn't have the time to talk to her right now so it would be better if she got out of his way. Maybe she could find a hotel in the town and stay there until the crisis was over? Now that she'd come all this way, she would prefer to get everything settled, but it wasn't fair to expect him to deal with the issue of their divorce when he had so much else going on.

'Nonsense! Of course you can't leave. You've only just got here.'

Seb's tone was brisk and her heart sank when she heard it. She didn't want to cause a scene but she knew it would be better if she left. Deciding to get divorced was a big step for any couple and they needed time to talk about what it entailed. She was just about to tell him that she would book into a hotel when the phone rang and she stopped as he picked up the receiver.

'Seb Bridges.'

Libby waited in silence while he listened to what the caller was saying. Even though she couldn't hear what was being said, she could tell it wasn't good news. He looked extremely troubled when he hung up.

'That was the coastguard again. Apparently, the tanker is carrying some sort of organic compound used to make pesticides. It's highly toxic and also believed to be carcinogenic even in fairly low doses.'

'Is it water soluble?' she exclaimed in dismay.

'They're not sure. However, in the absence of

any information to the contrary, we shall have to assume that it isn't. Which means if any of the containers rupture, the chemicals could be washed ashore.'

'It's a real nightmare scenario,' she agreed worriedly. 'It's coming up to the weekend and I expect a lot of people still use the beaches around here even at this time of the year.'

'And every single one them will be at risk if they come into contact with any of those chemicals,' Seb concluded, grimly.

Libby shivered. It didn't bear thinking about so she focussed on practicalities instead. 'Are you going to tell your staff?'

'Of course. They need to be fully informed about all the facts. One of our nurses has just found out that she's pregnant and I certainly don't want her coming into contact with a substance like that,' he said, heading for the door.

'Of course not.' She quickly stepped aside, shrugging when he paused beside her. 'I just wish there was something I could do to help.'

'If you mean that, I can easily find you a job. We're going to be really stretched when things start moving around here. Another pair of experienced hands would come in very useful.'

'Are you sure? You don't think it would be…well…*awkward* having me here?' she said doubtfully. It wasn't that she didn't want to help, because she did. She just didn't want to make his life any more difficult if he was involved with Cathy or some other member of the team. Her heart hiccuped painfully at the thought, but the truth had to be faced.

'Awkward?' He frowned. 'You're a first-rate doctor, Libby, and you know your way around an A and E unit better than most. Maybe you haven't worked in emergency care for a couple of years but you won't have lost any of your skills. You'd be doing me a favour if you agreed to help.'

'Thanks.' Libby smiled, deeply touched by the compliment. She'd often wondered if it had been a bone of contention between them that she'd decided to opt out of emergency care and go into general practice. However, there'd been nothing in his tone to indicate that…unless he no longer cared what she did, of course.

'I'll be happy to help any way I can,' she

said, determined not to let the idea gather momentum. They were heading towards a divorce so what difference did it make if he cared or not?

'Great.' He opened the door. 'I'll give you a quick tour so you can get your bearings. There's nothing worse than the sticky stuff hitting the fan while you're still trying to muddle your way around.'

'Like our first day at the Royal, you mean?' she said, and he laughed.

'Exactly like our first day at the Royal!' He grinned down at her, his hazel eyes warm with the memory. 'Remember when we were told to take that old lady for an X-ray? It took us half an hour to find the radiology unit!'

'And when we got there we discovered there were no radiographers on duty because they'd gone for lunch and we had to take her all the way back to Casualty.' She shook her head. 'You'd have thought someone would have warned us the department closed at lunchtime, wouldn't you?'

'Ah, but that would have meant them actually

helping us. We were trainees, don't forget. The lowest of the low. I can't remember anyone actually talking to us—they just snapped orders.' He smiled at her. 'It's a good job we had each other for support or we'd have gone completely mad!'

'Probably.'

Libby felt a sudden tightness in her chest and turned away, but the damage had been done. Remembering how close they'd been was just too painful when it only served to highlight how far apart they'd grown in recent years. As she followed Seb through the unit, she found it hard to concentrate on what he was saying. What did it matter if the state-of-the-art radiology department came complete with its very own CT scanner? And why should she care if bloods were cross-matched in the unit's own lab? None of those things had any bearing on what really mattered, which was the state of their marriage.

When she had made her vows eight years ago she had meant them. She had promised to love Seb until she died and in her heart she had promised to love him long after that, too. Yet here she was, just biding her time until she could tell him that she wanted to renounce those vows, sever the bonds that joined them together. How could anything matter more than that?

'And last but definitely not least we have our very own theatre.'

Seb stopped so Libby could look through the glass panes set into the top of the doors outside the operating theatre. A wave of tenderness washed over him as he watched her stretch up on tiptoe so that she could see through the glass. He'd forgotten how petite she was and that she would have a struggle to see through the high windows.

His eyes skimmed over the gentle, womanly curves he knew so well and he felt another reaction occur in his body, one which had been all too predictable at one time. Libby's beauty and femininity had always affected him and little had changed in that respect, it seemed.

'It all looks very hi-tech in there.'

'It is.' Seb dredged up a smile as she turned to him. He couldn't afford to let her see the effect she still had on him. If she'd decided to end their marriage then he wouldn't try to make the situation more difficult for her. Even though it wasn't what he wanted, he wouldn't stand in her way if it was what she'd decided to do.

It was just too much to deal with that thought right then. He swung round and headed back the way they'd come. 'So now you know where everything is, don't you?'

'Yes. Thanks. I can see why you were so keen to take this job. It's one of the best-equipped trauma units I've ever seen.'

'It is.' He elbowed open the swing doors that separated the theatre suite from the rest of the department and held them while she passed through. 'There's no doubt that having the best equipment available really helps, but it would be worthless without the right staff. They're the ones who make the department what it is, and they're a great bunch of people.'

'Of course,' she agreed quietly.

Seb frowned. He couldn't help noticing that there had been a definite lack of enthusiasm about her response. It appeared that his comment about the staff had struck a chord, although he wasn't sure what chord that was. He was just about to ask her what was wrong when he thought better of it. There was no point asking questions when he might not appreciate the answers, was there? It was a relief when Jayne appeared to tell him that Ambulance Control was on the phone.

He quickly excused himself and went to the office, his heart sinking when the controller informed him that there'd been a massive explosion out at sea when the tanker had struck the gas rig. Despite everyone's efforts to evacuate the crews from both the rig and the tanker, there were multiple casualties, the first of which were being flown straight to the hospital.

Seb hung up and checked his watch against the helicopter's ETA. He had ten minutes to get things moving, ten minutes to get himself moving, too. Somehow he had to set aside this agony he felt about losing Libby and concentrate on what needed to be done.

He headed straight to Resus, knowing that the team would be in there. Nobody noticed him at first, then Gary spotted him and stopped talking and the others realised the time for action had arrived.

'The first 'copter is on its way in,' he said crisply. 'Three men with serious burn injuries. ETA approximately nine minutes now. Marilyn will head up one team, Gary the second and I'll take charge of the third.'

'Do we know how many casualties we're going to have to deal with yet?' Gary asked anxiously.

'No. But we'll think in double figures and that way it will be easier to move up or down the scale,' Seb replied, moving to the bed nearest to the doors. Cathy and Jayne would be working with him as usual, although if there was a chance that any of the casualties had come into contact with those chemicals, he would make sure Jayne was well away from the danger area. He didn't intend to put her unborn child at risk.

'If there's any sign of chemical contamination, I want you out of here,' he told her. 'Understand?'

He sighed when he saw the relief on her face as she nodded. It had been remiss of him not to have made that clear to her before. He'd been too caught up in his own problems to worry about how his staff were feeling and it was an oversight he wouldn't make again. Mistakes occurred when people were put under too much pressure so he had to forget about everything else and get on with the job.

The doors suddenly opened and he swung round, expecting to see the paramedics bringing in their first patient, but instead he saw Libby come in. All of a sudden he was overwhelmed by the sheer magnitude of what was happening. Libby wanted to end their marriage. She no longer wanted to be his wife—she wanted a divorce. Maybe he was guilty of burying his head in the sand, but he had never expected it would come to this!

'So what do you want me to do?'

She stopped in front of him and his heart

suddenly lifted in sheer relief when he heard what she'd said. Was she actually offering to reconsider her decision to leave?

'What would you like to do?' he murmured huskily.

'I don't mind. Whatever's the most useful, basically.' She glanced round the room and shrugged. 'I don't mind acting as gofer. You'll need someone to take blood samples to the lab for cross-matching, and fetch drugs—things like that. I'm happy to do it if it will help.'

'Right, thanks. I'll bear that in mind.'

Seb dredged up a smile but he could feel it *inching* its way out of his boots. He knew that all they were doing was putting off the inevitable. She wanted a divorce and all she had to do now was to tell him that.

The doors crashed open again and this time it was the paramedics with their first patient. Seb told them to bring the trolley over to him. It took just a few seconds to transfer the man onto the bed and a couple more to set things in motion. This was the easy bit, of course, doing the job he'd been trained to do. The hard bit would come later, after his work here was finished.

Pain lanced through him once again. Nothing he'd ever learned had prepared him for the agony of losing Libby.

CHAPTER FIVE

Friday: 7 p.m.

'I NEED another line putting in, stat! Libby…?'

'Got it.'

Libby reached for a fresh cannula and ripped open the package. She swabbed the patient's arm then swiftly inserted the needle into a vein. His whole system was closing down as shock from the injuries he'd suffered took its toll, but the needle slid into place at her first attempt. She smiled to herself. It was good to know that she hadn't lost her touch in a crisis.

'Thanks. Now squeeze that fluid through as fast as you can go. We're going to lose him if we're not careful.'

Seb barely glanced at her as he carried on removing a sliver of metal from the injured man's throat, but she didn't need mollycoddling. Far from delegating her to the role of helper, he had involved her at every stage and she had to admit that it felt good to be able to use her old skills again. She began rhythmically squeezing the bag of saline, knowing how important it was to get the life-giving fluid into the man's system so that it would help to compensate for all the blood he was losing.

'Damn!' Seb cursed softly as the razor-sharp sliver of metal slid through the forceps he was using. She could see the frustration on his face when he looked up 'There's so much blood about that I can't get a grip on it.'

She saw him take a deep breath before he returned to the task, and smiled to herself. She couldn't count the number of times she'd seen that happen. Seb was incredibly tenacious when presented with a seemingly hopeless situation. He never gave up and would fight, tooth and nail, if he thought there was a chance of saving a patient's life. If anyone could save this man's life, it would be Seb.

'Got it!'

He let out a little whoop as the lethal sliver came free. Cathy quickly swabbed the area before he set to work again—sewing up the severed artery with a skill that many surgeons would have envied. He'd had his choice of specialities after he'd qualified and could have gone into any number of disciplines, including surgery, but he'd always loved the pace and uncertainty of trauma care. Seb thrived on the unknown and the risky, whereas she preferred the familiar and the routine. It was another area in which they differed greatly.

Libby hurriedly pushed that thought to the back of her mind because she didn't want to think about things like that at the moment. The bag of fluid had almost run through but before she could change it, Sarah, their haematologist, arrived with a supply of whole blood. Libby had to admit that she was impressed by the speed with which things moved in the unit— bloods were cross-matched seemingly in minutes, X-rays ready to be viewed in seconds. Compared to the last A and E department she'd worked in, it was another world and she could understand why Seb had been so enthusiastic when he'd been offered the post as consultant here.

'Right, that's all I can do for him. It's up to the surgical team now. Can you give them a call, Jayne, and tell them we're sending another one up to them?' Seb stripped off his plastic apron and gloves then glanced across the room. 'How many is that so far? I hope someone is keeping count.'

'Too right we are,' Marilyn piped up from the next bed. 'Young Gary and I have a bet on as to how many folk we get to patch up tonight. My guess is fifty, although junior here reckons it's going to be nearer the hundred mark.' Marilyn shook her head. 'That's the trouble with these young guys. They overestimate the size of *everything*!'

Everyone laughed, even Gary. Libby smiled, too. There was a wonderful rapport between the members of the team and that undoubtedly helped them work so well together. She couldn't help comparing it to the stuffy approach of her colleagues in the practice

where she worked. There was very little camaraderie there, sadly.

'I think we've earned a break before the next
batch arrive.'

She looked up in surprise when she realised
that Seb was speaking to her. 'I'm quite happy
to stay on here if someone else needs a break.'

'Thanks, but that's not the way we do things.'
He glanced at the two nurses. 'I want you both
to take a break now. The canteen is open so
make sure you get something to eat.'

Cathy and Jayne didn't quibble as they left
Resus together. Libby frowned as she glanced
at the other teams who were still working on
their patients. 'Don't you want to give them a
hand first?'

'There's no need. They know what they're
doing and they're more than capable of doing
it, too.'

Seb urged her out of the door, sighing when
he saw how reluctant she was to leave. 'Trust
me, Libby. I know what I'm doing. A major
incident like this is extremely stressful for
everyone concerned, so you need to recharge

your batteries whenever you get the chance. This could go on throughout the night and we need to be able to treat the patients with the same degree of care and attention whether they're the first to arrive or the last.'

'You really think it will go on for that long?'

'Yes, I do. This is just the tip of a very big iceberg so let's prepare ourselves for the long haul, shall we?' He led her to the lift then grinned at her. 'I don't know about you but I'm starving.'

'I wouldn't mind a cup of coffee,' she admitted.

'I thought so. What time did you leave Sussex today? It must have been around lunchtime, I imagine.'

'I set off straight after morning surgery finished. I had a half-day owed to me and decided to take it today so I could drive up here.'

Libby stepped into the lift, feeling suddenly nervous. There had been too much going on before to talk about the reason for her visit, but now it seemed that they had some time to themselves.

'You made very good time. It's a long drive, especially on a Friday when there are so many people trying to get away for the weekend.'

Seb pressed the button for the sixth floor then leant against the wall. His eyes were hooded, making it difficult for her to guess what he was thinking. Was he waiting for her to bring up the topic uppermost in both their minds, or did he prefer to make small talk until after the emergency was over?

It was impossible to decide so in the end she took the coward's way out. Maybe she should have got it over with while she had the chance but she couldn't quite bring herself to say the words that would effectively end their relationship. It seemed too cold and too clinical to talk about it here in the lift so she would wait until later.

'The motorway was really busy but the traffic wasn't too bad once I left it.' She shrugged, hoping that he would follow her lead and let the subject drop for now. 'Thankfully, I'd just got here when the storm broke otherwise that would have delayed me.'

'It's been a bad one,' he agreed, straightening

up as the lift came to a stop. He put his hand on the small of her back when she hesitated after they got out. 'The canteen's this way.'

Libby didn't say anything as he guided her along the corridor but she was absurdly conscious of the pressure of his hand on her back. Her cotton blouse provided very little protection. She could feel his strong fingers resting against her flesh and a tide of heat suddenly rose up inside her as she recalled all the other times when she had felt them on different parts of her body…

'Here we are.'

Seb let her go so he could open the door to the canteen. Libby scurried through it as though pursued by a horde of demons. She could feel her pulse racing as the blood surged though her veins and she bit back a groan of dismay. It had been *ages* since she'd reacted this way around him. The physical side of their relationship had gone the way of the rest and it had been months since they'd made love. How ironic it was that today of all days she should suddenly remember how wonderful their sex life had been!

'What can I get you?'

Seb waited while Libby sat down at a table in the corner he had chosen for them. It had been a deliberate decision to sit there because it would afford them some privacy.

'Just coffee will be fine, thanks.'

'Are you sure?' He drummed up a smile, determined not to let her know how difficult this was for him. He didn't want to talk about getting divorced, today or any other day. Although he knew how far apart they had grown in recent months, he'd always assumed that they would be able to work through their differences somehow or other, the 'other' being that Libby would decide to move north to be with him.

Now he could see that it had been his biggest mistake. He shouldn't have let matters lie, let them fester. He should have told her that he loved her and wanted her, but instead he'd allowed his pride to get in the way. Now he was going to pay the ultimate price for his arrogance and he could only hope that he and his pride would be very happy together.

'How about a sandwich to go with that

coffee?' He managed to hold the smile, although it felt as though his emotions were being forced through a shredder and spat out at the other side. 'It's going to be a long night, and if you're serious about staying on here to help then you'll need something to sustain you.'

'Of course I'm serious about helping,' she said sharply. 'Why shouldn't I be?'

'No reason at all. Sorry.' Seb held up his hands, palms out, in the universal sign of surrender, and she sighed.

'I'm sorry, too. I didn't mean to snap at you like that. I'm just a bit on edge…' She broke off, obviously thinking better of what she'd been about to say.

Seb hastily turned away. He certainly didn't want to encourage any revelations if they had to do with the dire state of their marriage. 'I'll fetch you a sandwich then you can decide if you want to eat it or not,' he said as he beat a retreat.

He sighed as he tagged onto the end of queue by the counter. He was starting to feel like the cowardly lion in the *Wizard of Oz:* always running away instead of facing up to any danger. However, at some point during the weekend he would have to pluck up his courage. He and Libby were going to get divorced. There! He'd managed to think the unthinkable and now all he had to do was to learn how to live with it.

He bought a ham sandwich for Libby and a double portion of shepherd's pie for himself plus drinks then went back to their table. It was break time for those on night duty so the canteen was crowded and he saw several people glance their way. He knew most of the staff at the Grace Darling Hospital by now and they knew him, too, so no doubt his marital status had been picked over and discussed many times.

How would they feel if they knew what was really going on tonight? he wondered as he unloaded the tray. Would they sympathise with him or with Libby? Should he have moved here to fulfil his dream of running a top-flight trauma unit, or should he have stayed in Sussex and saved his marriage? Should Libby have given up her job and moved here with him, or had that been expecting too much?

He had no idea whose side these people would take if it came to a choice between him and Libby—hell, even *he* wasn't sure if he would take his side any more! How could a job—*any* job, his or Libby's—compare to the life they'd once planned together?

Maybe they were both to blame for what had happened. They had lost sight of the important issue, which was their love for each other. If they had put that first then the rest might never have happened. Now it would be almost impossible to get back to the point where it mattered more than anything else. Somewhere along the way their love for each other had been relegated to second place and he had a horrible feeling that was where it was destined to stay.

CHAPTER SIX

Friday: 8 p.m.

'TREATMENT room. There'll be someone there to take the patient from you.'

Libby stepped aside as the paramedics rushed the trolley into the building. She moved to the next ambulance and climbed on board so she could make a quick assessment of the patient. They'd had over thirty casualties brought through the doors so far and there were still a lot more to come.

The fire which had engulfed the tanker and the gas rig had injured many people. They were being brought ashore by the air-sea rescue teams, as well as by local fishermen who had responded to the mayday call the coastguard had put out. She had been doing triage since she'd got back from her break—sorting out the most severely injured so they could be treated first. It was quicker if she did the job outside so she was meeting the ambulances as they arrived. Now she nodded as the paramedic finished reciting a list of the drugs the patient had received on his way to hospital.

'Take him to the cubicles and tell the staff that he's a priority three.'

'Does that mean I'm at the end of the queue, Doc?' Despite the burns to his hands and his face, the man managed to grin at her. 'Story of my life, that is. I'm always at the back when they're giving anything out!'

Libby laughed. 'In this instance, it means you're a winner. The more severe your injuries, the higher up the list you go.'

'I'd better not complain, then.' The man sobered. 'I saw the state of some of my mates and I wouldn't want to trade places with them, I can tell you.'

'I know.' She patted his shoulder. 'We're doing everything we can for them.'

'I know you are. Thanks.' He smiled as the

paramedics slid the trolley out of the ambulance. 'OK, guys. Wagons roll!'

Libby sighed as she climbed out of the ambulance. The bravery that had been displayed that night had been truly moving. It wasn't just the helicopter rescue crews, although they certainly deserved a special mention. It was the men who'd been working on the rig, too. She'd lost count of the number of times a patient had told her that he owed his life to his workmates.

'How are we doing out here?'

She swung round when she heard Seb's voice and felt a little thrill run through her when she saw him standing by the main doors. She'd seen very little of him since they'd come back from the canteen—he'd been working in Resus while she'd been outside. However, during that time, he'd never been very far from her thoughts.

'Not too badly,' she said, going over to him. She pushed back the hood of the fluorescent yellow raincoat she'd been given to wear, and shivered when a few drops of rain trickled down her neck.

'You're frozen!' he exclaimed in concern. 'Do you want to swap with one of the others? I can send Jayne to relieve you if you've had enough of getting soaked.'

'No, it's fine. I just had a drip trickle down my neck—that's why I shivered.' She eased her finger inside the collar to wipe away the vexing droplets, and he grinned.

'You never did like the rain very much, did you?'

'Not when it's trickling down my neck,' she retorted, hunching up to see if that would help her to get at the dribble.

'Here, let me do that for you.' Before she knew what was happening, his hand slid inside the collar of her coat. 'Remember the time we hired that cottage in Wales and it rained non-stop for the whole weekend?' he said, running his fingers over the damp patch of skin just below her nape.

'I…um, yes. The weather was dreadful, wasn't it?' she said, hoping he wouldn't notice the slightly breathless note in her voice. He was only trying to help her, she told herself sternly, but it was no good. The feel of his fingers rubbing her skin was too enticing; she could feel ripples of sensation spreading from the spot where he was touching her and running through the whole of her body.

'I would never have believed it could rain so hard if I hadn't seen it for myself.' He chuckled, his hand stilling for a moment as he glanced down at her. 'We were so wet, in fact, that the tips of our fingers actually started to shrivel!'

'Not an experience that I'm eager to repeat,' she replied tartly, and he laughed.

'Me neither, although there were some good moments, as I recall.'

'I'm afraid I only remember how wet it was.'

She stepped away from him, running the zip right up to the top of its track, although it was a bit like bolting the stable door after the horse had fled. Now that Seb had touched her, he was unlikely to do it again but she didn't intend to take any chances.

She cleared her throat, striving for a casual tone, but it wasn't easy to achieve it when her body was tingling from both the touch of his hand as well as the resurgence of old memories. Although the weather had been atrocious, it hadn't spoiled the weekend. They'd been working so hard in the months leading up to it that it had been wonderful to finally be able to spend some time together.

Tears suddenly stung her eyes as she remembered how they had made a huge fire in the living-room grate and sat in front of it, toasting bread for their tea. It had been such a little thing yet it seemed to sum up the wonder of their relationship. They hadn't needed expensive meals or exotic holidays: they'd only needed to be together. What a shame it was that they had allowed themselves to lose sight of that one simple fact.

'So do you want to carry on out here, or do you want to swap places with Jayne?' Seb's tone was polite almost to a fault but it didn't fool her. He knew what she'd been thinking because he'd been thinking about it, too.

'I'll stay out here for a bit longer.'

Libby swung round before he could say anything else. There was no point thinking about all the good times they'd had—it would only make it harder for both of them. Those days were in the past and it was the present she had to concentrate on now. However, knowing that she wasn't immune to him made her feel very vulnerable indeed. A shiver ran through her as she recalled how it had felt when he had wiped away that drop of water. One touch and it seemed that she was like putty in his hands!

Her face flamed as she hurried over to the next ambulance. The paramedics greeted her with a smile, unconcerned that she was a stranger to them. There were a lot of staff from other departments working there that night so they had no reason to wonder who she was or what she was doing there. They didn't know that she was Seb Bridges's wife, come from Sussex to ask her husband for a divorce, neither did they care. They just wanted to get the job done with the least amount of hassle possible.

Libby took a deep breath then squared her shoulders. She would follow their example and get through this night the best way possible, too. And, once it was over, she would get on with her life.

Seb went back to Resus and checked the X-rays that had appeared on the computer in his absence. His patient, Brian Johnston, had multiple fractures: both femurs, left tib and fib, pelvis.

Seb logged them up, one after the other, using them to blot out everything else. He wouldn't think about the way Libby had reacted to his touch just now. He wouldn't worry about what it had meant, or if it hadn't meant anything. He wouldn't even think about that weekend in Wales and how wonderful it had been to spend the time together. He would think about his patient and how he could help him because it was the only way he would survive this increasingly stressful night.

'How's his BP?' he asked as he went over to the bed.

'I've seen better.' Cathy pulled a face as she glanced at the monitor.

Seb frowned as he turned to look at it, too. The

patient's BP was in freefall, plunging faster than a runaway lift. 'Looks like internal bleeding to me. Have you spoken to the surgical team?'

'Yes. All the theatres are in use at the moment. Our guys hope to finish up in about twenty minutes' time, barring any mishaps,' Cathy explained.

'He won't last for twenty minutes. At this rate his BP will be through the floor in five. Get another line into him while I check those X-rays again. I'd prefer to know where the bleeding is coming from rather than play take my pick.'

He went back to the computer. Reading an X-ray was a skill in itself, and with so many and so varied injuries it was difficult to decipher exactly where the bleeding might be coming from. He leant forward and stared at the shot of the patient's pelvis. Was there a faint shadow around the pubic symphysis which could indicate internal bleeding?

'Have a look at this, would you, Ben?' he said, calling over the radiologist. He pointed to the screen. 'Does that look like a shadow to you?'

'It could be.' Ben took off his glasses and bent until his nose was almost touching the screen. He was extremely short-sighted but his skill at deciphering an X-ray was second to none. 'It's worth taking a closer look, if you want my opinion,' he said finally, popping his glasses back on.

'That's good enough for me.' Seb clapped him on the shoulder then went back to the bed. Marilyn had just despatched her patient to the assessment ward so he beckoned her over. 'I might need a hand here, if you wouldn't mind.'

'Your wish is my command, master,' she said cheerily, and he rolled his eyes.

'I don't think! Being at the beck and call of any man definitely isn't you, Marilyn.'

'Sadly, it isn't.' She grinned at him, although he was surprised to see a hint of concern in her eyes. 'I just thought it might give you a bit of a boost if I was suitably obsequious.'

'Oh, and why should I need a boost, pray?' he retorted, gloving up. He ran a quick mental checklist of his options and decided that the most likely source of the bleeding was the bladder. And if the bladder had been ruptured then not only would it need to be stitched up but both the abdominal and pelvic cavities would need to be flushed out to stave off infection caused by the leaked urine. Talk about one thing leading to another!

'Because you're looking a bit down in the mouth this evening.' Marilyn's voice was muffled as she pulled a fresh plastic apron over her head. However, he could see the curiosity in her eyes when she emerged. 'Did you know your wife was coming up for a visit?' she asked with seeming innocence.

Seb wasn't fooled by it. He knew that Libby's arrival had caused a stir. Although he liked and admired his team, considered them as friends even, he couldn't bring himself to discuss his private life with them. Not yet. Not until the Ts were crossed and the Is were dotted and divorce was spelled out in the letter which would arrive shortly from Libby's solicitor…

'No. It was a complete surprise to me.' He caught himself up short. There was no need to get too far ahead, was there?

'A pleasant one, I assume,' Marilyn said lightly, stripping open a sterile pack of surgical instruments and laying them on the trolley.

'I'm always pleased to see Libby,' he said, relieved that he didn't have to pretend to tell the truth. Marilyn was far too sharp to try and fool her with a pack of lies—she would have seen through them in an instant. And said so, too, because she wasn't someone who minced her words either. It was a double relief when he saw from her expression that he'd managed to convince her that everything was fine between him and Libby.

Of course, the time would come when he would have to tell people what had really happened, but not yet. For now he could carry on as though everything was normal and that he wasn't about to face the most horrendous experience of his life. He could talk about Libby as his wife, be with her, share this night with her, and maybe in some small way it would help to prepare him for what was to come.

He took a deep breath and forced the feeling

of despair right to the very pit of his stomach. He just had to get through this night and in the morning he would deal with whatever happened the best way he could.

CHAPTER SEVEN

Friday: 9 p.m.

'DR BRIDGES is in Resus. Can I ask him to phone you back?'

Libby had been passing the office when she'd heard the telephone ringing. The flow of casualties had increased to a flood in the last hour and the trauma unit was starting to look like a war zone. There were injured people lying on trolleys and slumped in chairs. She'd been working in the treatment room since she'd come back inside—stitching cuts, covering burns and generally making herself useful. They had run out of dressings so she'd been on her way to fetch a fresh supply when she'd stopped to answer the phone. Now she frowned when she heard what the caller was saying.

'Can you hold on?' she said quickly, knowing that Seb would want to deal with this himself. 'I'll see if Dr Bridges can speak to you now.'

She hurried out of the office and went straight to Resus. Seb was standing by the bed nearest to the door, and her heart ached when she saw how tired he looked. There were deep lines pulling down the corners of his mouth and heavy shadows under his eyes. Was it just the strain of keeping on top of the job that was taking its toll? Or the fact that he'd guessed why she had come to see him?

'Problems?' he asked, turning towards her.

'Could be.' She forced the thought to the very back of her mind. She'd spent months wondering what she should do and now she needed to resolve the issue and move on. Maybe Seb would be hurt but he would get over it in time. She would, too. People got divorced every day of the year and they survived. She and Seb were no different to them.

'The coastguard's on the phone. It turns out that the captain of the tanker had his wife and his son on board with him. One of the local fishermen picked them up but now he's got problems—his engine has packed up. He's had to drop anchor while he tries to repair it and he's just radioed through to say that the boy is ill. He thinks it might be appendicitis.'

'Can't someone else bring the child ashore?' Seb queried, frowning.

'No. The helicopters are still ferrying the injured from the rig. The storm is getting worse and they don't think they'll be able to fly for very much longer.'

'What about the other boats in the area? Can't they help?'

'The fishing boat drifted off course when its engine failed and the coastguard doesn't want to send another boat out to it. Apparently, the rig is so unstable that they think it might collapse so their main priority is to get the crew off before that happens.'

'Hell!'

Seb ran a weary hand over his face. Libby could tell that he was working through the problem, trying to find a solution. She wasn't surprised when he suddenly strode to the door. If anyone could come up with an answer to this dilemma, it would be Seb, she thought proudly.

'I'll have a word with the coastguard and find out what options we have—if any.'

'Thanks.'

Libby followed him out of Resus, feeling her heart beating in jerky little thuds. She knew that she shouldn't feel like this about him, shouldn't feel proud or impressed, but she couldn't help it. She did admire him and always had. He would go to any lengths if it meant he could help someone in need and never gave any thought to himself. Although in the beginning the attraction she'd felt for him had been very physical, it had soon deepened into something more. She'd loved his spirit as well as his body, loved everything he was and strove to be. Nobody who loved Seb could love just one side of him; they *had* to love the whole.

Tears glistened in her eyes as she made her way to the office. She didn't want to have to face facts like that but she couldn't ignore them. Maybe they had grown apart but on some deeper level she knew that part of her would always belong to him.

'Is there any chance that you could patch me through to the fishing boat? I need to decide how urgent the situation really is.' Seb beckoned her into the room when she hesitated in the doorway. He put the receiver back onto its base and switched on the speaker so that she could listen to the conversation as well.

Libby went and sat down beside the desk, clasping her hands tightly together in her lap to stop them trembling. She mustn't think about herself any more. She must focus on what was happening—someone else's tragedy.

'My name is Sebastian Bridges and I'm a trauma specialist at the Grace Darling Hospital. Am I speaking to the captain?' Seb said clearly, once the connection had been made. He carried on once the man had confirmed his identity. 'Good evening, Captain. Can you update me on the boy's condition?'

Libby leant forward as she struggled to hear what the captain was saying. It was a very bad line and his voice kept fading but from what she could gather, the child was in a bad way. She glanced at Seb and could tell how worried he was.

'How long ago did he stop complaining about the pain?' he asked when the captain paused. He looked very grim when the man explained that it had been over an hour since the child had told them that his tummy didn't hurt any more. 'I don't like the sound of that. It's more than likely the appendix has perforated, in which case he needs urgent medical treatment. Do you have any idea when your engines will be fixed?'

Libby held her breath as she waited for the captain to reply. If the appendix had perforated then the boy could be in grave danger. Once the contents of the appendix were released into the abdomen, peritonitis would soon set in, so her heart sank when the captain explained that it would be several hours before he was able to get the engines working again.

'We can't delay that long,' Seb said bluntly. 'The boy needs to be treated sooner rather than later if he's to survive. Is there any way of getting me out to the boat?'

The coastguard came back on the line at that point and they spent a couple of minutes discussing the problem. When Seb hung up everything was arranged. The off-shore lifeboat would ferry him out to the fishing boat then it would bring him and the boy back to port. However, the thought of him going out in the storm was more than Libby could bear and she jumped to her feet as he hurried to the door.

'I'm coming with you!' She saw him stop and knew he was going to refuse to let her go with him so quickly forestalled him. 'You'll need someone to assist you and it would be easier if I went along instead of one of the others. They're far more use here.'

'I really don't think it's good idea,' Seb began, thinking that had to be the biggest understatement of all time. The thought of Libby putting herself at risk by going with him made him feel positively queasy, but he could tell from the look she gave him that she wasn't going to be deterred.

'Nonsense! It's the only sensible solution. You know it is!'

Her beautiful mouth pursed with annoyance

and he had to swallow his groan of dismay. He didn't want to have a stand-up fight with her but he knew how tenacious she could be once she made up her mind.

He shook his head, equally determined to get his own way. 'I'm sorry but the answer is still no. You aren't on the staff here, Libby, and it would be totally unethical to allow you to accompany me.'

'I never took you for a coward, Seb,' she said quietly, her blue eyes meeting his in a look that made heat unfurl in his stomach. On the surface, they might be arguing over whether or not she should be allowed to go with him, but underneath the argument was raging on a wholly different level. Did she really see him as a coward? Did she think he was too scared to admit that he was to blame for ruining their marriage?

He swung round, not wanting her to know how much the suggestion hurt him. 'I'll be leaving in five minutes' time. If you want to come, meet me at the main entrance. If you're not there, I'll go without you.'

She didn't say a word as he left the office and

he was grateful for that. He didn't need his nose rubbed into the mess he'd made of his life. Once upon a time he'd had everything a man could wish for: Libby and a job he loved, a future that combined the two. After tonight was over, he'd just have his job and it could never compensate for all that he'd lost.

His love for Libby had been the bedrock on which he had founded all his dreams. Every dream he'd had had been more special, more wonderful, because she had shared it with him. Now she would have her own dreams, separate to his, her own life in which he wouldn't play any part. There would no longer be that unique bond between them, that invisible link that had made him feel so special. Without Libby's love, he was just a man. With it, he was someone out of the ordinary. He didn't know how he was going to live without her but he would have to learn. It was too late to do anything about it…

Wasn't it?

Seb's heart began to pound with renewed vigour. *Was* there a way to change her mind? He had no idea, quite frankly. It all depended on how Libby felt about him and he had no idea about that either any more. At one time he could have confidently claimed that she adored him, but they had moved so far beyond that point now that it was like looking back through the wrong end of a telescope. Those idyllic days were mere pinpricks on the horizon of his memory, although they hadn't disappeared completely from sight.

He could still remember how it had felt to love and be loved with such intensity, and it seemed inconceivable that all that feeling could have disappeared completely. Surely there must be something left, even a smidgen? A tiny flicker of that love which he could nurture and help to grow strong again? If he could persuade Libby to give them a second chance, they might they be able to recapture what they'd had in the past.

Seb drew himself up. He knew there was no guarantee that she would be willing to try again but it was worth considering the idea. Somehow, during the next few hours, he had to find the time to fan those flames and rekindle her love for him. Come the morning, Libby was going to leave him for good, unless he found a way to stop her.

CHAPTER EIGHT

Friday: 10 p.m.

'THERE it is—over there!'

Libby pointed through the windscreen as she spotted the sign for the lifeboat station. She could feel her tension rising as Seb headed towards it. The weather was atrocious and the thought of going out to sea in such appalling conditions wasn't a pleasant one, but she'd come this far and she had no intention of backing out at this stage. When Seb parked the Land Rover and jumped out, she quickly followed suit, gasping when a gust of wind almost blew her off her feet.

'Careful!' Seb grasped hold of her arm and held onto it as they made their way to the boat. They had to walk along quite a narrow stretch of the harbour wall so she didn't try to pull away. One glance at the churning black water below them was enough to deter her from reclaiming her independence. Anyway, it was reassuring to have him there beside her. She always felt so much safer when he was around.

She sighed softly. Totting up all the reasons why she liked being with Seb certainly wouldn't help when the time came to tell him that she wanted a divorce. She slipped out of his grasp as they reached the lifeboat and was relieved when he didn't appear to notice. There was no point making herself any more vulnerable than she already was.

'Hi! I'm Seb Bridges and this is Libby.' Seb kept the introductions brief. 'The coastguard should have told you we were coming.'

'They did indeed.' The coxswain shook their hands then glanced behind him at the boat. 'We're ready whenever you are, Doc, so climb aboard.'

Libby's eyes widened as she got her first real look at the lifeboat. She wasn't sure what she'd been expecting but it was definitely something more substantial than this bright orange craft.

'Don't judge the little lady by her looks, Libby.' The coxswain grinned when he saw the shock on her face. 'She's a lot more stable than she might appear to the untrained eye.'

'I certainly hope so.' Libby summoned a smile as she made her way on board. Another member of the crew led her aft of the wheelhouse and helped her to put on a life-jacket. There were seats in there so once she was kitted up she sat down. From this position she had a good view of the wheelhouse and she could feel her stomach churning with apprehension as she watched the coxswain and another crewman start the engines.

'These guys are experts, Libby—they know exactly what they're doing.' Seb finished fastening his life-jacket and sat down beside her. Reaching over, he squeezed her hand. 'It will be fine—you'll see.'

'Tell me that again when we're back on dry land,' she replied pithily, and he laughed.

'You're not a scaredy cat, are you?'

'Yes, I am.' She looked past him at the view out of the porthole and shuddered. 'I never was all that fond of the sea even on a good day.'

'It's not too late to change your mind.' Seb leant forward so that she was forced to look at him and she could see real concern in his eyes. 'Nobody will blame you if you decide not to go, sweetheart.'

'Maybe they won't, but I'll blame myself.'

She removed her hand from his grasp and gripped the edge of her seat instead. She didn't look at him again as the boat set off because she knew it would be a mistake. It had been a long time since he'd called her by that tender endearment and she didn't want him to know how much it had affected her. Once upon a time she *had* been his sweetheart, the person he'd loved most in the world. How tragic it was that all that love had amounted to nothing.

Despite the turbulent seas, the lifeboat made excellent time. In a remarkably short time, Seb could see the lights of the stranded fishing boat up ahead. The coxswain turned to him, raising his voice to make himself heard over the throbbing of the engines.

'I'll bring her alongside then we can transfer

you to the fishing boat. Are you both going, or is Libby staying here?'

'It's up to you, Libby. Do you want to go or not?'

Seb deliberately opted for a bland tone, although he knew that it might be too late for that. He hadn't meant that endearment to slip out and certainly didn't intend to compound his error by repeating it. He might still think of her as his sweetheart but it had been obvious from her reaction that she didn't consider him in the same light.

'I've come this far so I may as well go the whole way.' She gave him an equally bland smile in return. 'I don't want anyone thinking that I'm too scared to finish the job.'

'Fine.' Seb didn't argue with her. It was up to her what she did, as she was making perfectly clear.

He stood up as the crew brought the lifeboat alongside the fishing boat. There was a heavy swell running and the two boats were bobbing up and down like corks on water. He had no idea how they intended to transfer them from one vessel to the other until one of the crew went to the forward cabin where all the rescue and maintenance equipment was stored and re-appeared with a rope and pulley.

He and Libby followed the men on deck and waited while they attempted to pass one end of the rope to the crew on the fishing boat. It took a couple of tries but once the line had been secured at both ends, they were ready to go.

'Right, Doc. You and Libby are going to be transferred via this harness.' The coxswain showed them a padded harness which was attached to the line by a series of metal buckles. 'It's quite simple really—we strap you both into this then haul you across the gap. There's a stretcher which we'll send across once you're safely on board—the kid can be transported back on that.'

'It sounds easy enough in theory,' Seb said, guardedly.

'It is. It might be a bit hairy but console your-selves with the thought that we've not lost anyone yet,' the coxswain told them cheerfully.

'Now, if you and Libby could stand, facing one another, we'll get you kitted up.'

Seb waited while the harness was slipped over their heads and secured under their arms. Various buckles and straps were fastened then checked. He breathed in deeply to settle his nerves because this was a first for him, too. Tension suddenly gripped him as he inhaled the familiar scent of Libby's perfume. It shouldn't have been possible to distinguish it from the smell of brine and diesel, yet even at such a fraught moment he was aware of anything that had to do with her.

'It might make it easier if you two wrap your arms around each other,' the coxswain advised them. 'There's bound to be a lot of buffeting about from that wind and it will help to sta-bilise you.'

Seb felt heat suffuse him as he put his arms around Libby. 'Like this?' he said, hoping that nobody would suspect the effect it was having on him to hold her that way. It had been far too long since they'd been this close and his body was revelling in the feel of hers.

'Yep, that's fine. Now, if you could grab hold of the doc's waist, Libby… That's better.'

The coxswain moved away and for a moment they were alone together. Seb looked down into her face and forced himself to smile. 'Are you OK?'

'Fine.'

Her tone was clipped but it didn't fool him. She was just as aware of his nearness and the thought made his heart run wild for a moment until sanity prevailed. He had no way of knowing if she was aware of him in a good way, did he? Maybe she hated being this close to him, loathed the feel of his arms around her? Where once he would have known instinctively how she was feeling, he was no longer sure.

Did his touch arouse her to passion or fill her with disgust? Did it do neither because she was indifferent to him? Seb swallowed his sigh of regret. He would have dearly loved to know the answers to those questions but he wasn't privy to that kind of information any more. Whatever Libby felt, she was keeping it to herself!

Libby could feel her heart pounding. She

knew it was partly from fear of what was about to happen, but mainly because of Seb's nearness. Feeling his strong arms around her was sheer torture, even though she had lain awake far too many nights, wishing he was holding her. When the coxswain shouted to tell them that they were ready to start, she sucked in her breath. She just wanted to get this over!

The harness tightened around them and the next moment they were lifted off their feet. Libby cried out when she saw the deck being replaced by swirling black water. The wind was incredibly strong, battering them about as they swayed on the end of the line, and she whimpered in terror.

'Hang onto me,' Seb shouted in her ear. 'You'll be fine.'

She didn't need to be told twice; she clung to him as they bounced and swayed across the gap between the boats. The whole trip could have lasted only a couple of minutes at most but it felt like an eon had passed before she felt the deck under her feet. Seb quickly undid the harness and helped her out of it then followed the captain below decks.

'The youngster's in here with his mum,' the captain told them, leading them through a tiny galley into the crew's sleeping quarters. Libby could see a young boy lying on one of the bunks and just one glance was enough to tell her that he was in a very bad way. His mother was kneeling beside him and she immediately stood up when they appeared.

'I'm a doctor,' Seb told her as they hurried forward. 'I need to examine your son.'

'Yes, yes, please, hurry,' she replied in heavily accented English.

Libby smiled her thanks as she knelt down beside Seb. The boy was barely conscious and he was burning up with fever. When Seb folded back the blanket and gently examined him, he moaned in pain.

'It looks as though peritonitis has set in,' Seb said quietly, moving out of the way so she could examine the child herself.

Libby frowned as she gently palpated the boy's abdomen. 'The muscles in the abdominal wall are in spasm and there's definite signs of bloating, isn't there? I wouldn't have expected to find symptoms like these after such a short space of time has elapsed, though.'

'It's possible the appendix ruptured earlier than we thought it had. There's that honeymoon period after it perforates when the patient is free from pain and that's when a lot of people think the problem has righted itself.' He shook his head. 'Sadly, that doesn't happen. It's imperative that we get him to hospital. The longer we delay, the greater the danger he's in.'

'We need to get some antibiotics into him. Maybe we can set up a drip as soon as we get him back to the lifeboat. I don't want to waste a second more than we have to, do you?'

'No, I don't.' He stood up and turned to the captain. 'The coxswain is sending over a stretcher—can you get it down here? The child desperately needs to be in hospital so we'll take him back with us.'

Libby turned to the boy's mother as Seb finished speaking. 'We're going to take your son to hospital,' she explained gently, seeing the fear on the other woman's face. 'He's a very sick little boy and he needs urgent medical treatment. Do you understand what I'm saying?'

'*Da!* Yes.' The woman nodded. 'Yuri said he had pain but I did not listen. It is all my fault…'

She broke into a storm of anguished weeping. Libby patted her arm. 'It's not your fault. It's just one of those awful things that happen and now we have to make sure that Yuri gets the best possible care.'

The poor soul didn't look convinced but Libby couldn't spare any more time to reassure her. The captain had fetched the stretcher now so she and Seb got the child ready then a couple of the crew carried him on deck. Fortunately the rain had stopped but the sea was still very rough, huge waves tossing both the boats around. It wouldn't make the transfer any easier so it was decided that she would go first and Seb would follow with the stretcher.

Her stomach was churning with nerves as he helped her into the harness. It was one thing to make the journey with Seb and another thing entirely to do it by herself. She was trembling by the time he had finished checking that everything was securely fastened and couldn't hide her trepidation from him.

'You'll be fine, Libby. You've done it once and you can do it again,' he told her firmly.

'I hope so…' She trailed off, not needing to hear the quaver in her voice to prove just how scared she was.

Seb pulled her to him and there was a look in his eyes that made her heart race even faster, although not from fear this time. 'You will be fine,' he repeated, his deep voice grating. 'I won't let anything happen to you. That's a promise.'

Before she realised what he intended, he bent and kissed her on the mouth. She just had a moment to savour the salty coldness of his lips before he stepped back. The next thing she knew, she was flying up into the air and Seb was staring up at her…

Libby closed her eyes. She didn't want to see the angry waves beneath her or the hunger in Seb's eyes. She wasn't sure which scared her most. If she fell into that water, she would drown. If she went back on her decision to ask him for a divorce, the strain of continuing their sham of a marriage would slowly suck the life out of her. The only way she would survive was by standing firm, but it wasn't easy when her heart was telling her that she shouldn't go through with it. Surely it would be better to have just a bit of Seb's love instead of having none at all?

CHAPTER NINE

Friday: 11 p.m.

'How's he doing?'

Seb crouched down beside the stretcher and checked that the cannula was still securely taped to Yuri's arm. The lifeboat was bouncing around so much that it was difficult to maintain his balance. He gritted his teeth when they hit another huge wave. The sooner they were back on dry land, the happier he'd be, although it wouldn't do a lot to address his own problems.

'He seems a bit more comfortable now.'

He steeled himself when Libby glanced up and their eyes meshed. What was she thinking? he wondered as he searched her face. Had he upset her by that kiss, or didn't she care?

She'd always been so open with him in the past, yet she seemed to have put up an invisible barrier between them now. It scared him to know that she was distancing herself from him this way when it would make it that much harder to win her back.

'Amen to that,' he said, determined not to let her know how worried he was. He looked round when the coxswain tapped him on the shoulder, doing his best to behave as though this was just an average night in his week. It was, in fact, the worst night of his entire life, but if he gave in to this panic that was churning inside him, he might never recover.

'The coastguard has just radioed to say that there's an ambulance standing by at the harbour,' the coxswain informed him. 'We should reach port in just under five minutes' time.'

'Thanks. And thanks again for everything that you and the rest of the guys have done tonight. I know what a hectic time you must have had and I really appreciate what you did by ferrying us out there.'

'All part of the service, Doc. Anyway, talking

about busy nights, I don't imagine your night's been a picnic.'

'It certainly hasn't,' Seb replied with a touch more fervour than he'd intended. He cleared his throat when he saw Libby glance at him in surprise. 'We'll get the boy ready for transfer to shore.'

'If you need a hand, just say the word.'

The coxswain returned to his post. Seb helped Libby check that the straps on the stretcher were all securely fastened. They entered the harbour basin and he breathed a sigh of relief. Just a few more minutes and they would be on their way to the hospital. The rescue mission had gone a lot more smoothly than he'd dared hope it would, although what was going happen during the rest of the night was anyone's guess.

He glanced at Libby and felt panic grip him again. Could he persuade her to give their marriage another chance? It all depended on whether or not she thought it was worth saving and that was something he couldn't foretell. The thought of how this night could end was almost more than he could bear, but he had to stay strong if he hoped to win her back. He had to fight for the woman he loved and the life they could have together. Maybe it was a battle he wouldn't win but it wouldn't be for want of trying, so help him!

'Careful!'

Libby grabbed the end of the stretcher as it dipped dangerously close to the water. Even though they were back in port, there was a heavy swell running and transferring the boy from the boat to dry land was a difficult manoeuvre. She looked round in relief when Seb took the end of the stretcher from her.

'You jump ashore. It's too much for you to try and lift this stretcher out of here.'

Libby did as she was told because it was simpler than arguing and causing a delay. Anyway, it wasn't as though he was casting aspersions on her ability to do the job—he was merely looking out for her, as he always did.

Heat rushed up her face at the thought and she quickly made her way to the ambulance.

She'd met the crew earlier that night when they had delivered several patients to the trauma unit and they greeted her like an old friend.

'So this is what you lot in Trauma get up to, is it?' the younger of the two male paramedics said with a grin. 'While we're slaving away at the sharp end, you get to go on a nice little boat trip?'

'I don't know about a *nice* little boat trip,' she retorted. 'How would you fancy being pegged onto a line like a piece of wet washing and getting hauled across between two boats with your feet dangling in the water?'

'Sounds like a doddle compared to what we have to put up with, doesn't it, Jim?' the paramedic said, winking at his partner. He sighed gustily. 'Some people have all the luck. They get the treats while the rest of us end up doing all the hard graft.'

'And I don't think!' Libby replied, laughing. She glanced round when she heard footsteps on the gravel and realised that Seb had arrived with the stretcher. She moved out of the way while the paramedics lifted it into the back of the ambulance. The stretcher belonged to the lifeboat so they moved the child onto the trolley and handed it back to one of the crew then Seb climbed into the ambulance to check how their patient was doing.

'How is he?' she asked anxiously.

'Much the same.'

His tone was clipped and she frowned because she had no idea why he sounded so uptight all of a sudden. Now that the really dangerous part of the exercise was over, he should be feeling pleased about how well it had gone, yet there was a definite edge in his voice when he addressed the paramedics.

'Take him straight to hospital. I'll meet you back there.'

'Right you are.' The younger paramedic glanced at Libby. 'Do you want a lift back…?'

'My wife will be travelling back with me,' Seb said curtly, cutting him off in mid-sentence.

The paramedic didn't say anything else, but Libby could tell how awkward he felt as he hurriedly closed the ambulance doors. Seb didn't say another word as he strode over to his car but she was fuming as she followed him. He had—quite deliberately—made sure the other man knew that she was his wife and that he should stay well away from her!

'There was absolutely no call for that,' she said, getting into the passenger seat. 'You had no right to make that guy feel so uncomfortable. He was only trying to be helpful.'

'He was hitting on you, Libby. You know that as well as I do so please, don't act the innocent because it won't wash.'

'He wasn't hitting on me! He was just being…pleasant.'

'Then I apologise.' Seb swung the car round and his expression was grim. 'Obviously, I was mistaken.'

'Yes, you were,' she said firmly, although she wasn't so sure any more. It had been a long time since she'd flirted with a man and she couldn't be certain of reading the signs correctly. Since she'd met Seb, she had never looked at anyone else and had never wanted to, but after they were divorced, everything would have to change. If she didn't want to spend the rest of her life on her own then she would have to start dating again. A couple of her friends from med school had got divorced and remarried in the past few years, yet she simply couldn't imagine doing the same thing herself.

She sighed softly. The trouble was that she couldn't picture herself with any man other than Seb. She couldn't imagine sharing the same kind of closeness they'd enjoyed with anyone else. Seb had always been her soul mate, the person who had understood her best. Could she ever find that kind of intimacy again?

She didn't think so, yet the alternative—a life lived on her own—wasn't a prospect she relished. Somehow she was going to have to pick up the pieces after the divorce and learn to live without him. After all, she'd got through this past year so now it was just a case of hanging on until the pain passed. One day, in the hopefully not-too-distant future, she would find someone else to love, although deep down she knew that she would never love anyone as much as she'd loved Seb.

* * *

'Thanks. I really appreciate this.'

Seb dropped the phone onto its rest and stood up. He had just persuaded the surgical team to squeeze Yuri into their very long list. He made sure one of the nurses would tell Yuri's mother when she arrived, that her son would be undergoing an appendicectomy and that afterwards he would be admitted to the paediatric unit. With a bit of luck the boy would make a full recovery so that could be classed as one positive result at least. Heaven knew, he needed some good news tonight.

After he briefed the nurse he then went to check how his team were faring. Marilyn greeted him with a smile when he went into Resus.

'Aha! The wanderer returns. So how did it go?'

'Not too badly, all things considered.' Seb looked around, his brows rising when he saw that all the beds were empty. 'What have you done to all the patients? I thought you'd be snowed under by the time I got back.'

'In other words, you thought we couldn't manage without you?' Marilyn laughed as she stripped off her apron and rolled it into a ball.

'Sorry to disappoint you, boss, but you aren't indispensable.'

'So I gather.' Seb tried to keep any inflection out of his voice but the comment had touched an already raw nerve. He wasn't indispensable when it came to his job or his marriage, apparently.

He gave himself a quick mental shake. Sinking into an abyss of self-pity certainly wouldn't achieve anything. 'What's the tally so far, then?'

'Fifty-three and counting,' Gary chipped in from the sinks, where he was scrubbing his hands. 'One of the paramedics reckons this is merely the lull before the storm and that we'll get a lot more customers before the night is over.'

'Then I reckon you two should grab a few minutes to yourselves while you can. I'll take over in here while you have a break.'

'I'd do the noble thing and argue, only my feet are killing me,' Marilyn observed wryly, making for the door. 'I'll be in the rest room so just shout if you need me.'

'I will,' Seb promised, as she and Gary disappeared.

He took a deep breath after they'd gone, relieved to have some time on his own at last. It had been non-stop since the coastguard had first contacted them and he could do with a breather, too, although he would stay in Resus where it was quiet. If he went to the rest room then he would have to talk to people and it was the last thing he felt like doing.

He decided to check through the case notes to get an overview of how the night had gone so far and switched on the computer. A lot of the cases had been fairly routine—burns, abrasions, lacerations—but he took the time to read through each case. Everything hinged on statistics nowadays and if he hoped to get extra funding, he needed the right ammunition to back up his demands. He had just closed down the system when the door opened and Libby appeared.

Seb's heart began to pound. He knew immediately that the moment he'd been dreading had arrived. He didn't say a word as she came towards him—he couldn't. He felt like a condemned man about to meet his fate—completely powerless to stop what was happening. She stopped in front of him and his heart beat even faster when he saw the determination in her eyes. He knew then that nothing he said or did would stop her going through with it.

'I've put this off for as long as I can, but I need to talk to you, Seb.'

'Libby,' he began desperately, even though he knew he was wasting his breath.

'Don't.' She held up her hand and there were tears in her eyes. 'There's no point saying anything, Seb, because I've made up my mind. I want a divorce.'

CHAPTER TEN

LIBBY felt as though she could barely breathe. Even though she had been building up to this moment all day long, it was still a shock to hear herself say the words out loud. All of a sudden she was beset by panic. What if she was making a mistake? What if Seb agreed to the divorce and it wasn't what she truly wanted?

'It really isn't the right time to talk about this, Libby.'

Seb's tone was harsh and she flinched. She could see how grim he looked as he got up and walked to the door. She knew that he was going to leave before she could say anything else and the thought of having to go through this all over again was more than she could stand.

She hurried after him. 'Wait! You can't walk out on me like this. We need to talk…'

'What is there to talk about?' He swung round and her heart ached when she saw the hurt and the anger in his eyes. 'You've just told me that you've made up your mind that you want a divorce, Libby. It doesn't sound as though there's much I can say to dissuade you.'

She wasn't sure what to say in her own defence and shrugged. 'I don't want you to dissuade me. I just want us to deal with this the best way we can.'

'And so we shall. But not here and not now. OK?'

He opened the door and this time she didn't try to stop him leaving. There was no point. If she had made up her mind about the divorce then he had made up his mind that he wasn't going to talk about it at the moment. Maybe he was right, too. There was a lot they needed to discuss and it would be better if they talked in private.

She followed him out of Resus, uncomfortably aware that she'd made a complete mess of things. Cathy was coming out of the cubicles and she stopped when she saw them walking along the corridor.

'I was just about to page you,' she said to Seb. 'There's a patient I'd like you to see.'

'Of course.' Seb headed towards the cubicle then paused and glanced back. Libby shivered when she saw the chill in his eyes. 'The rest of the team are taking a break so why don't you join them? I'll give you a shout if I need you again.'

'Thanks,' she murmured, refusing to let him see how painful it was to be treated that way. She sighed as he disappeared into the cubicle because how else did she expect him to treat her after what had just happened? They were no longer a couple, a pair, but two people poised on the brink of leading separate lives. Maybe they had been living apart for almost a year, but it would be vastly different after their divorce was finalised. Legally and morally they would be free of the bonds of marriage. It was what she'd wanted when she had set out that day yet the thought filled her with a sudden sense of dread. She couldn't imagine ever being completely free of Seb.

* * *

'He's going to need dialysis to give his kidneys time to recover. Can you get onto the renal unit and see if they have a bed available? If they haven't, he'll need to be transferred to another hospital.'

Seb left Cathy to make the arrangements and went to speak to the patient's wife. Mike Buchanan was an engineer on the gas rig. He'd been injured when one of the metal supporting struts had fallen and trapped him beneath it. Although the X-rays had shown no sign of any fractures, there was extensive muscle damage. His right leg was badly swollen, his blood volume had fallen and there was a definite rise in the amount of urea and potassium in his blood. It was a classic case of crush syndrome and could prove fatal if Mike wasn't treated quickly enough.

Mrs Buchanan was in the relatives' room. There was quite a crowd in there because a lot of family members had rushed to the hospital when news of the incident had been broadcast over the radio and television networks. Seb escorted her outside, seeing the dread on her face. She obviously feared the worst so he wasted no time in reassuring her.

'Your husband is alive and we're aiming to keep him that way,' he said firmly, guiding her into an alcove so they could have some privacy.

'Oh, thank God!' Tears welled to her eyes and he patted her arm.

'Mike isn't completely out of the woods, though, I'm afraid. He suffered extensive muscle damage when he was trapped beneath a girder. That has led to a condition known as crush syndrome, whereby large amounts of protein pigments are released into the bloodstream from the damaged muscles and prevent the kidneys from functioning properly. He's going to need dialysis until his kidneys recover so I'm trying to get him a bed in the renal unit here.'

'But he'll be all right after that?'

'There's a chance that his kidney's might not recover fully but I'm hopeful that we've caught it in time.' He smiled at her, doing his best to appear upbeat. 'We just have to keep our fingers crossed for now.'

Seb showed her to the cubicle so she could

sit with her husband then went to see how Cathy had fared. Fortunately, the renal unit was able to offer them a bed so he signed off Mike Buchanan and left Cathy to organise the transfer. The queue in Reception had thinned dramatically so he hoped that they were nearing the end of the really busy period. There were bound to be more casualties brought in but with a bit of luck the worst might be over.

The thought had barely crossed his mind when Gary came chasing after him. Seb groaned. 'What's happened now?'

'One of the search and rescue helicopters has crashed. There's no more details yet but it came down on the outskirts of town. There were three crew on board plus another three guys who they'd rescued from the tanker.'

'Let's just hope it hasn't hit any of the houses,' he said fervently, heading straight to Resus. Marilyn was already there and Jayne, although there was no sign of Libby, unsurprisingly enough. He knew he'd been rather hard on her before but even though he'd guessed what had been coming, it had been a shock to hear her say the word divorce. It was a moment that would be forever imprinted on his mind, like their wedding day. He could recall everything that had happened on that day, too—how beautiful Libby had looked and how happy she'd sounded—and it was the worst kind of torment to compare the two events. It made him see how hard it must have been for her to tell him about her decision and he was instantly contrite. He'd had no right to treat her that way.

'Anyone know where Libby has got to?' he asked as casually as he could because he didn't want his team to know how wretched he felt.

'She's left,' Marilyn informed him cheerfully. She frowned when she saw the shock on his face. 'Didn't she tell you she was leaving?'

'I...um... Yes, of course, she did. I just wasn't sure if she'd already gone or not.'

Seb turned away, making a great production of taking a fresh pair of gloves out of the dispenser to give himself time to think. Libby had left the hospital and every instinct was telling him to go after her and apologise for the way he had behaved, but how could he? He couldn't desert his post because his marriage was on the rocks. He had to stay until this incident was over. And by that time, she could be miles away.

He groaned under his breath. What a mess this was turning into!

Libby leant forward and peered through the windscreen. Surely she should have seen a sign directing her towards the motorway by now?

She slowed as she came to yet another junction and was forced to face the fact that she was lost. She must have taken a wrong turning after she'd left the hospital and now she had no idea where she was heading—except that it was away from Seb.

A sob caught in her throat but she forced it down. There was no point crying. The whole reason she'd decided to leave had been so she could stop herself getting upset. She and Seb needed to discuss their divorce calmly and rationally, and it was too much to expect that they could do that tonight. It would be better if she let him mull over her decision—he would realise then it was the only solution. They needed to cut their losses and move on, and hopefully he would come to understand that himself.

The thought of him coming to terms with their divorce unsettled her so she hurriedly dismissed it. At the present moment she had a more pressing problem to worry about, namely in which direction she should be heading. She pulled over to the side of the road and checked her map. She was just trying to work out which way she should go when there was a deafening noise overhead. It sounded very much like a helicopter passing over her, although she had never known one to fly so low.

Rolling down the window, she peered out and gasped in horror when she saw the helicopter just skim the tops of the trees near to where she was parked. It disappeared from view and a moment later there was a tremendous crash and the whole sky suddenly lit up.

Libby's hands were shaking as she started the car and pulled out onto the road. She couldn't believe that another disaster had occurred tonight of all nights. She could see people running out of the houses that lined the road so she followed them and soon found herself on the edge of a playing field. The helicopter had crashed into some trees that bordered the field and it was now on fire. There was no way of knowing how many people had been on board but she could see several bodies lying on the ground.

She parked her car and grabbed her medical bag out of the boot. A crowd was already gathering and she had to push her way through them. She ran over to the first of the casualties and knelt down beside him. He was unconscious but breathing so she placed him in the recovery position then called over one of the bystanders and asked her to stay with him. There was another man lying on the ground a few feet away so she ran over to him. A police car had arrived now so she quickly explained that she was a doctor when one of the officers came over to her then carried out a rapid examination, but there was nothing she could do for the man: he was dead.

'There's another guy over here, Doc. He's one of the crew and he's in a really bad way.'

Libby snatched up her bag and followed the policeman to the edge of the woods. She could feel the heat that was coming off the helicopter as it burned and sincerely hoped there wasn't anyone left inside. Kneeling on the ground, she took a quick look at the man and felt her heart sink when she saw the piece of metal that was sticking out of his side. He was conscious and obviously in a lot of pain, but he still managed to speak to her.

'Have they got everyone out? I tried to land but the main rotor had packed up…'

'Shh. Don't worry about that now. Just lie still while I check you over.'

She carefully examined the wound but it was impossible to tell how deeply the metal had embedded itself into his flesh. She glanced at the police officer and shook her head when she saw the question in his eyes. 'I can't do anything for him here. He needs to go to hospital. Are the ambulances on their way?'

'I hope so, but it's been a bit hectic tonight and there's no way of knowing how long it will take them to get here.'

Libby didn't say anything as she opened her bag—she'd seen at first hand how stretched the emergency services had been. Her job now was to make the patient as comfortable as possible and hope that help would arrive sooner rather than later.

She gave the pilot a shot of morphine to ease the pain then left him in the care of another of the onlookers. There were three more men to see and they had a variety of injuries ranging from fairly superficial cuts to extensive burns. She did what she could but she was very aware how little it was. What they really needed was someone with specialist skills to deal with their injuries, like Seb.

Her heart bunched up inside her because it wasn't just the casualties who needed Seb. She needed him, too, needed him there to reassure her that she was doing all she could to help these poor people. She also needed him because of who he was—the man she loved with all her heart—and it was a shock to face up to her true feelings when she had tried so hard to bury them.

She still loved Seb and probably always would love him. It was living with him that had proved to be so difficult, or rather living without him. These past twelve months had been the worst time of her entire life and that was why she had decided to end their marriage. She couldn't keep on living this way—neither really married nor single. Either Seb wanted her with him or he didn't, and he'd made his choice when he had moved here and left her behind.

Tears pricked her eyes but she had accepted the truth some time ago and nothing had changed. Seb didn't want her any more and she mustn't make the mistake of thinking that he would change his mind.

CHAPTER ELEVEN

Saturday: 1 a.m.

'THIS is Alistair Roberts—the pilot of the helicopter that crashed.'

Libby rattled out the information as the stretcher was rushed into Resus. Seb did his best to follow what she was saying but it wasn't easy. Having her reappear like this was the last thing he'd expected to happen. It took every scrap of will-power he could summon to keep his mind on the job.

'How much pain relief has he had so far?' he rapped out as the paramedics lined up the trolley beside the bed.

'Ten milligrams of morphine administered just over half an hour ago,' she explained crisply. 'Plus another five milligrams on board the ambulance.'

'Fine. Let's give him another five milligrams before we move him onto the bed.' He turned to the patient. 'We're going to get this over as quickly as possible, Alistair, but it's still going to be uncomfortable, I'm afraid.'

'I understand,' the man muttered.

Seb waited while Marilyn administered the drugs. The paramedics had placed the patient on his left side so that the shaft of metal wouldn't be forced deeper into the abdominal cavity. However, he knew they would have to proceed with the utmost caution. Seb turned to his team, his gaze lingering on Libby before he forced himself to get a grip.

'We need to be ultra-careful when we move him onto the bed. No sudden movements, guys—just nice and smoothly does it.'

Everyone nodded, including Libby, but he didn't allow himself to wonder if it meant that she intended to stay and help. It was up to her if she decided to stay, although if he'd had any choice in the matter, he wouldn't have let her leave again…

'Seb?'

He jumped when Marilyn reminded him that everyone was waiting for his instructions. 'On my count,' he said firmly. 'One, two, three.'

They moved the patient onto the bed with the minimal amount of fuss. 'I want a second line put in,' Seb instructed. 'And a urinary catheter, too.'

He left the nursing staff to get on with their jobs while he concentrated on his own. He did a quick primary survey—airway, breathing, circulation—then checked the actual site of the injury. The metal spike had entered the body on the rear right-hand side, just above the right kidney. This type of wound was associated with injuries to the retroperitoneal organs—the colon as well as the kidney and the lumbar vessels. More rarely, it could cause damage to the pancreas, aorta and inferior vena cava, so his number-one priority was to find out what they were dealing with. Then, as soon as he was happy that the patient was stable, he would hand him over to the surgical team.

He called Ben Robertson over and asked him to do the X-rays then put a call through to Theatre. Everything had to be done a step at a time, which could be frustrating. However, he'd learned by experience that it paid to be patient sometimes. Rushing in headlong often made a bad situation turn out even worse.

His gaze went to Libby, who was setting up a second intravenous line, and he sighed. He should have applied that dictum to his own life. If he'd stopped and considered the damage he'd be doing by taking this job, he might not be in this position.

Libby moved out of the way while the radiologist set up his equipment. The X-ray machinery was mounted on ceiling tracks and all it took was a few touches of the various buttons to position it over the bed. Everyone moved out of the way while the films were taken and when they returned to their posts, she didn't go with them. There was very little she could do now for the pilot. Once Seb had established the extent of his injuries and stabilised him, he would be rushed to Theatre. She was, in effect, surplus to requirements, yet for some reason she felt reluctant to leave and resume her journey home.

It had been wrong of her to drive off like that, she admitted as she slipped out of the room. She should have waited until Seb had finished work then gone back to his house with him. They needed to sort things out and it would be better if they did it themselves rather than employ a third party. Once their solicitors became involved, the matter would be taken out of their hands, and she hated the thought of a group of strangers ending their marriage for them. She and Seb had made the decision to marry and they should be the ones who ended it.

She made her way to the rest room. There was nobody in there so she had the place to herself for once. She filled the kettle then sat down and waited for it to boil. She felt bone-tired and depressed now that the adrenaline rush that had kept her going while she'd been helping the helicopter crew had disappeared. It was a feeling she remembered only too well from the time she'd spent working in Accident and Emergency after she'd qualified. It was one of the reasons why she'd decided to go into general practice, in fact. She'd hated the emotional ups and downs of the job, although Seb had thrived on it. He seemed to come into his own when he was under pressure and the thought made her feel more depressed than ever. No wonder they had drifted apart when they were such opposites.

The kettle came to the boil so she made herself a cup of coffee and curled up in a chair. The coffee was far too hot to drink so she put the cup on the floor and closed her eyes. She would stay at the hospital until Seb had finished then go home with him and sort everything out. There really was no point prolonging their agony.

'Take him straight through to Theatre. We've done all we can and now it's up to the surgical team.'

Seb stripped off his gloves and tossed them into the bin. The X-rays had shown extensive solid organ injury. Although the right kidney had escaped damage, the head of the pancreas and duodenum had been penetrated. Add that to tissue and nerve damage and he didn't rate the pilot's chances very highly.

For some reason, the thought depressed him more than it normally would have done, and he sighed because he understood why. Every setback he encountered from now on would seem so much worse now that there was nothing to counterbalance it. Whenever he'd felt downhearted about his job in the past, he'd thought about Libby and that had always lifted his spirits, but he wouldn't have that in the future, would he?

'It looks as though you've lost the proverbial pound.'

He glanced round when Marilyn came over to him, unable to raise enough energy even to pretend he was fine. 'I wish it was just money I'd lost.'

'Are you and Libby going through a rough patch?' Marilyn asked, lowering her voice so that the rest of the team wouldn't hear her.

'We've been through the rough patch and now we're on the other side...the place that leads in just one direction.'

'Surely things aren't that bad?' Marilyn exclaimed.

'Trust me—they are.'

He didn't say anything else. Although he knew he could trust Marilyn to be discreet, it felt wrong to discuss his marital problems with someone else—although maybe that had been his biggest mistake. Maybe he should have sought help instead of hoping that the problems would somehow magically disappear?

He frowned as he left Resus. It was something he hadn't considered doing before, but he should have done. If he and Libby had had counselling, they might have been able to work through their problems. Maybe he should suggest it to her now and see how she felt about the idea?

It was worth a try, he decided as he went in search of her. There was no sign of her in the treatment room or the cubicles so he went to the front desk to see if the reception staff had seen her recently. He drew another blank, which was rather a mixed blessing—at least she hadn't left, although he still had no idea where she'd gone.

He checked the office next but it was empty. He was just about to head up to the canteen to check there too when he realised that he hadn't looked in the rest room. He muttered a silent prayer as he opened the door, and was rewarded when he found her curled up, fast asleep in a chair.

Seb crept into the room and sat down, feeling a whole range of emotions wash over him. It was a long time since he'd seen her like this. The last time he'd driven down to Sussex they had ended up arguing and he had driven home again the same night. They hadn't spent a night together for almost a year, in fact, and that had been another major mistake, of course.

How could a marriage survive when there was no physical contact between a couple? It wasn't just sex—important though that was—but the small intimacies which were so vital to a healthy relationship: a hug, a loving glance, a gentle touch.

There'd been times early on in their marriage when they hadn't had the time to make love. Working the kind of impossible hours expected of a newly qualified doctor had left them little room for a private life, but they had got through that period by showing in small ways how much they had cared for each other.

When had they stopped doing that? he wondered sadly. When had they stopped making the effort? It didn't make any real difference now but he wished he could remember exactly when the intimacy had ceased. Reaching out, he stroked her cheek, feeling his heart aching with regret. He should have made sure that she knew how much he loved her!

'I'm so sorry,' he whispered. 'So very, very sorry for letting you down.'

'Seb, have you got a minute?'

He looked round when the door suddenly opened and Cathy appeared. 'Problems?' he said, standing up. Libby hadn't moved and he doubted if she was aware that he was there, which probably wasn't a bad thing. He was feeling far too emotional at the moment and he couldn't afford to feel this way if he hoped to convince her that their marriage could work if she'd only give him a second chance.

He had to be focussed, centred, he thought as he followed Cathy out of the door. He had to present the idea of them trying again to her with confidence and assurance so that she would believe it was worth taking the risk. He knew it was a lot to ask and that he didn't deserve another chance after the mess he'd made of things, but he couldn't just let her go without a struggle. He needed her, wanted her, loved her, and, by heaven, he was going to tell her that before this night was over. He wanted his wife back for keeps!

CHAPTER TWELVE

Saturday: 2 a.m.

LIBBY opened her eyes as the door closed. Her heart was racing as she sat up. What had Seb meant, that he was sorry for letting her down? Could it mean that he had been having an affair?

Pain ripped through her and she put her hand over her mouth to stifle her sob. Her legs were trembling as she stood up, but she couldn't stay there in case someone else came in and found her in this state. Picking up her cup, she took it over to the sink and emptied the cold coffee down the drain. She had just finished when the door opened again and Gary appeared.

'Having a quick cuppa?' he said cheerfully, heading for the kettle.

'Yes.' Libby dredged up a smile. She didn't want to believe that Seb had been seeing someone else, but what other explanation could there be for that apology? Pain ripped through her again and she hurried on, terrified that she was going to break down. 'How's it going out there? Have things settled down now?'

'They had—until the coastguard phoned to say that the lifeboat has just picked up some more members of the tanker's crew.' The young registrar grimaced. 'Apparently, they'd been ordered to abandon ship before it hit the rig but their dinghy was swept away. That's why they weren't found until now.'

'Are they badly injured?' she asked, because it was easier to think about someone else rather than worry about herself and Seb all the time.

'Two of them are in a pretty bad way, from all accounts. The rest have minor cuts and burns supposedly, although we can't be sure exactly what we're dealing with until they get here.' He groaned when the wail of a siren heralded the arrival of an ambulance. 'That was quick! Bang goes that cuppa I promised myself.'

'You have your tea and I'll cover for you.' She hurried on when he started to protest. 'While I can't claim to possess your level of expertise, I did a stint in A and E a few years back so I should be able to manage until you've finished.'

'If you're sure you don't mind?' Gary beamed when she shook her head. 'Then thanks. Tell Seb I'll be along in a few minutes, though, won't you? I wouldn't want him to think I'm shirking!'

Libby assured him that she would pass on the message and left. The first ambulance had drawn up outside by the time she reached Reception so she waited by the desk to see where she could be most usefully employed. Seb came hurrying out of Resus and he frowned when he saw her standing there.

'Don't feel that you have to help, Libby. You've done more than your fair share tonight.'

'I'm covering for Gary while he has a break,' she explained, hoping he couldn't tell how painful it was to wonder if he'd found someone to replace her. Was it someone from work, like Cathy for instance? Or someone from outside the field of medicine? She wanted to know, yet at the same time didn't want to hear anything about the woman who had supplanted her in his affections.

'Oh, right. Well, thanks.' He looked round when the doors opened and the patient was rushed in. 'Resus,' he ordered, after just one glimpse of the man's injuries. He turned to her. 'If you could cover the treatment room, it would be a big help.'

'Of course,' she agreed, moving away.

'Libby.'

She stopped when he called her back and a shiver ran through her when she saw how serious he looked.

'Maybe we can talk after the rush is over? There's a lot of things we need to sort out.'

He hurried away before she could say anything. Another ambulance arrived just then so she tried not to think about what she and Seb had to say to each other as she went to meet it. The patient had cuts on both his hands, although he appeared otherwise unharmed, so she told the paramedics to take him straight to the treatment room. He didn't speak any English, which made communicating with him rather difficult, but she managed to make him understand that she was going to treat his injuries.

Once she had cleaned and sutured the cuts, she took him to a side room and left him there to wait. Accommodation had been found for the tanker's crew and he would be taken there as soon as the mini-bus came back from delivering the last group of men. In the meantime, she gave him a cup of coffee then went to see her next patient, a young boy of sixteen who had suffered extensive burns to his forearms. Jayne had been delegated to help her and she sighed when she saw the extent of the teenager's injuries.

'Do you want me to call the burns unit?'

'Please.' Libby sighed. The paramedics had covered the boy's arms with gel packs to cool and protect the flesh from infection, but they were full-thickness burns and far too severe for her to treat. 'This is beyond my capabilities, I'm afraid.'

'Always best to know when you're beaten,' Jayne replied cheerfully, picking up the phone.

Libby didn't reply. The nurse couldn't have known that her comment would touch a nerve, but it had. Although she and Seb had tried to make their marriage work, they'd been beaten, too. Now it was time to let go of the past and move on. However, knowing that Seb might have found her successor was extremely painful. It made her see that moving on was going to be a long and difficult process, and that there was no guarantee that she would succeed.

All of a sudden she found herself wishing that she'd done something to stop what had been happening. Instead of waiting for Seb to come to her, she should have gone to him! She should have fought to save her marriage and not let her stupid pride get in the way. Now it was far too late to change things—unless a miracle happened.

'If we're all agreed, I'll call a halt.'

Seb looked at the people who were gathered

around the bed but there was no sign of dissent. They all knew that it was pointless to carry on trying to resuscitate the patient. With third-degree burns covering almost seventy per cent of his body, it was a miracle that he had survived this long.

Cathy switched off the monitoring equipment as Seb moved away from the bed. Gary joined him at the sink, looking as downcast as Seb himself felt. Losing a patient—even one as badly injured as this one—took its toll on them all. It was the downside of working in trauma care, the part of the job he hated most. No wonder Libby had decided to switch to general practice. It took a particular type of mentality to deal with the highs and lows of working in emergency care, and she was far too sensitive.

The thought made him feel worse than ever. He hated to think that he had trampled over her feelings when he should have done more to protect her. It took a massive effort to pretend that everything was fine as he turned to Gary, but it was his job to keep up his team's spirits.

'What's the score now? How many patents have we seen?'

'Fifty-nine and holding.' Gary scooped a handful of soap from the dispenser and grinned at him, successfully distracted by the question. 'Looks as though I'm in line to win the bet, doesn't it?'

'It certainly does.' Seb drummed up a laugh. 'So the coffee's on you tomorrow in the canteen, I take it?'

'Coffee *and* cakes,' Gary replied breezily, as Marilyn came to join them. 'It's not often I get the chance to prove my superiority so I intend to celebrate the occasion in style!'

'We'll never hear the end of this,' Marilyn grumbled, nudging Seb aside so she could reach the taps. 'OK, I admit it—you were right and I was wrong. Happy now, junior?'

'Yes.' Gary laughed. 'And I'll be happier still when you cough up that fiver you owe me.'

Seb left them still bickering and went to check that everything was in order. Cathy had called in the porters to take the dead man to the mortuary. The police would need to be informed of his death so that his family could be told, so Seb left Resus and went to find the officer on duty. The policeman was just leaving the side room that had been set aside for the use of the tanker's crew; he came hurrying over when he spotted Seb.

'Do you know where the chap who was waiting for the mini-bus has gone, Dr Bridges? I was told he was waiting in there but there's no sign of him.'

'Sorry. I've no idea where he is.' Seb looked around but there were very few people left in the waiting room. 'Have you tried the lavatories?'

'No, not yet. Where are they?'

'I'll show you.'

Seb led him to the men's lavatories but there was nobody in there. They also checked the ladies' lavatories just in case but they, too, were empty. He frowned as he looked along the corridor. 'I've no idea where he could have got to. Who treated him, do you know?'

'That lady doctor...I think her name's Libby.'

Seb's heart gave a little lurch at the mention

of Libby. 'I'll see if she knows where he might have gone,' he offered, doing his best to maintain an even tone.

'Thanks.' The policeman sighed. 'The inspector isn't going to be too happy if our chap's gone AWOL. We're under strict instructions to keep an eye on the crew until Immigration has interviewed them.'

'He must be somewhere about,' Seb assured him, although the policeman didn't look convinced.

He made his way to the treatment room and found Libby in the process of cleaning up a cut on a man's arm. She glanced round when he appeared and he had to make a determined effort to rein in his emotions when he saw how tired she looked. 'Sorry to interrupt, but could I have a word with you outside, please?'

'Of course.' She put down the plastic forceps she'd been using and smiled at the patient. 'I'll just be a few minutes.'

Seb led the way to an empty cubicle and perched on the edge of the bed. Libby frowned as she followed him inside.

'Is something wrong?'

'We seem to have lost a patient. That guy who was supposed to be waiting for the mini-bus has gone missing. I don't suppose you know where he is, do you?'

'I've no idea. I told him to wait until someone came to collect him, although he might not have understood me. He doesn't speak any English, I'm afraid.'

Seb sighed. 'It could be a genuine mix-up, I suppose. Maybe he thought he should wait outside or something.' He stood up. 'I'll go and see if I can find him before that policeman starts a full-scale alert.'

'Shall I come with you?'

'No. There's no point us both getting soaked, plus you have a patient waiting, don't you?'

'Of course. Sorry. I should have thought of that myself,' she said stiffly, pushing aside the curtain.

'Hey, I wasn't having a go at you!' He turned her round to face him and sighed when he saw from her shuttered expression that it was pre-cisely what she had thought he'd been doing. 'I really appreciate everything you've done tonight, Libby. You've been a real help. Not many people would have mucked in and got on with the job like you've done.'

He ran his hands lightly up her arms, trying to control the rush of emotions that hit him when he felt the softness of her flesh beneath his palms. All she had on was a thin blue cotton blouse and he could feel the warmth of her skin flowing into his hands.

All of a sudden the air seemed to be charged with tension. He knew that he should let her go, but his body had a very different agenda. His hands ran down her arms once more and he felt her shudder. When her eyes rose to his face, he could see the same uncertainty mirrored in them that he felt, too. She wasn't sure if this was the right thing to do any more than he was...

He drew her to him, feeling the shudder that travelled through him when their bodies came into intimate contact: breast to breast, thigh to thigh. It was a foregone conclusion after that what would happen and he was powerless to stop it. Lowering his head, he kissed her on the mouth, wondering if his own helplessness might ultimately save him. If he let her know how much he loved her, surely it would make a difference to how she felt?

CHAPTER THIRTEEN

Saturday: 3 a.m.

LIBBY knew that she should stop what was happening but she couldn't seem to drag herself away from Seb. The kiss was so wonderfully potent that it seemed to have drawn all the strength from her body. She pressed her hands flat against his chest, feeling his heart thundering beneath her palms, and that was when the first doubt crept into her mind.

Was it passion that made his heart beat so fast or shame?

Her mind captured the thought and expanded on it. Seb had always possessed very strong principles and he wouldn't find it easy to live with himself if he'd been having an affair. Maybe he hoped to atone for his actions by salvaging their marriage, but was that what she wanted? Did she *really* want a relationship that was founded on guilt?

It was hard enough to make a marriage work when you loved each other, but if love had died, it didn't stand a chance of surviving. Oh, they could pretend that everything was fine—go through the motions—but underneath would either of them be happy with second best? She certainly wouldn't and she didn't believe that he would either.

She pushed him away and stepped back. 'I have to get back to my patient,' she said in a voice that sounded as brittle as glass. Maybe Seb truly believed that he was doing the honourable thing but she refused to compromise. Either he loved her or he didn't—the choice was simple.

'Libby, wait!' He caught hold of her hand and held it fast when she tried to pull away. 'I'm sorry if you're upset because I kissed you, but I'm not sorry about why I did it.'

'And why did you do it?' she challenged, swinging round to face him.

'You know why,' he said softly, his eyes holding hers. 'I did it because I care about you.'

'I see.' Maybe if he'd declared that he loved her with his whole heart, it might have worked. However, instead of a declaration of love, he'd come out with a milk-and-water statement to the effect that he *cared* about her! Anger rose inside her and she glared at him. 'I'd respect you more if you told me the truth.'

'What do you mean by that?'

'That you've been having an affair and that kiss was your way of...*easing* your conscience!'

'An *affair*?'

'Yes!'

She wrenched her hand away. She didn't want to hear anything else, certainly didn't want to hear any details. If there was some woman waiting in the wings, then she didn't want to know anything about her!

Seb didn't try to stop her as she hurried out of the cubicle and it just seemed to prove that she was right. If he wasn't having an affair, he would have made sure she knew that for a fact!

Tears spilled from her eyes but she brushed them away. She refused to make a spectacle of herself in front of the people Seb worked with—it would embarrass them and upset her even more. She would try to remain calm while she was here and especially when she and Seb sat down and discussed the terms of their divorce. The last thing she wanted was him feeling sorry for her. He'd tried to make amends once already and she didn't want him to try again so there'd be no tears, no kisses, no more physical contact at all. This really and truly was the end of their marriage.

Libby believed that he'd been having an affair?
Seb could feel his insides churning as he made his way to the front entrance. He couldn't seem to get his head round the idea that she thought he'd been seeing another woman. Didn't she know that she was the only woman he'd ever loved? Apparently not, if she'd come out with a ridiculous accusation like that!

He swore softly as he made his way outside. There were a couple of ambulances parked under the canopy, but he didn't go over to see if there was anything he could do to help. He needed some time to himself without having to worry about other people. So maybe he wasn't ill or injured but he was hurting all right. Libby thought that he could just switch his feelings on and off at will, did she? She believed that he could love her one minute and someone else the next? If that was the case then she couldn't have any idea what real love was all about, and that thought was the worst one of all. Had Libby ever truly loved him the way he loved her?

His throat tightened in agony and he had to force down the cry of anguish that ripped through him. Turning, he stared across the rain-soaked forecourt, looking for any sign of the missing man. Under normal circumstances, there would have been people about, even at this hour of the morning. However, with all casualties apart from those from the tanker and the rig being ferried elsewhere, the place was deserted. If the missing seaman was out there then he must be hiding, and the thought did little to soothe Seb's overwrought nerves. The last thing he needed was all the hullabaloo of a full-scale search!

He went back inside and tersely informed the policeman that he'd been unable to locate the missing seaman. The announcement resulted in a lot of anxious questions but he didn't have the time or the patience to answer them. He curtly suggested that the officer should contact the hospital's security staff and left him to get on with it. He was just passing the cubicles when Gary waylaid him.

'Have you got a minute?'

'Sure.' Seb stepped into the cubicle and ground to a halt when he discovered that Libby was also in there. 'What's this, then? Are you having a party in here?'

She flushed when she heard the sarcasm in his voice, although she didn't say anything. Seb sighed under his breath because there'd been no reason to speak to her like that. It was just the shock of discovering that she thought he'd been having an affair that was making him behave that way.

'I enlisted Libby's help in case she had any good ideas about what this could be,' Gary explained cheerfully, oblivious to any undercurrents. 'We're none the wiser, though, so see what you think it is. I assumed it was the result of a burn, but David tells me that he's had it for a couple of days now. It's got me well and truly foxed, I have to admit.'

Seb frowned as the registrar moved aside so he could see the huge blister on the patient's left foot. 'You haven't been in contact with any chemicals, have you?' he asked, mentally crossing his fingers. If any of the containers onboard the tanker had started to leak, the coastguard would need to be informed. Anyone coming into contact with the chemicals would be at risk so all the search and rescue teams would have to be warned the danger.

'No. I work on the rig and I was nowhere near the tanker when it hit us,' the patient assured him. 'And as the doc just said, I've had this for a few days now.'

'Have you had any other symptoms?' Seb asked, moving to the bed so he could examine the blister. It was several inches wide—covering almost the full width of the foot, in fact—and extremely deep. The skin surrounding it was heavily inflamed, too. He frowned as he tried to work out what might have caused it.

'I've not felt too good for almost a week now, to be honest. I've been vomiting and felt really nauseous the rest of the time, too. I also had a touch of the runs, which was why I asked to go on sick leave this morning.' The younger man sighed. 'I was waiting to be picked up when we were told about the tanker heading towards us. Another ten minutes and I'd have left.'

'Tough luck,' Seb observed sympathetically, wondering if it could be a friction blister.

'I thought it might have been caused by David's footwear,' Libby put in quietly. She shrugged when Seb glanced up. 'It's similar to the type of injury you get when you wear new shoes, although this blister is much bigger than any blister I've seen formed that way.'

'I was wondering that myself,' Seb admitted, trying not to make too much out of the fact that they were thinking along the same lines. She was an experienced doctor and it was only natural that she should reach the same conclusions as he had. There was no reason to think that it proved how in tune they still were.

He cleared his throat. 'It's sited in an unusual place, though. Most friction blisters caused by badly fitting footwear appear on the heels or the toes rather than on top of the foot, don't they?'

'Yes. But if it was a new boot, for instance, and laced very tightly, it could create pressure in that area,' she suggested.

'Hmm, that's true.' He glanced at the patient. 'Are we on the right track, do you think?'

'I don't think so,' the patient said slowly. He shook his head. 'OK, I was issued with a new pair of work boots a couple of weeks ago, but they didn't give me any trouble from the first day I got them. They only started to rub *after* the blister began to form, not before.'

'So we can rule out your footwear, from the sound of it,' Seb said, gently probing the blister with his gloved fingers. It was filled with fluid and looked ready to burst at any moment.

'Ouch!' David winced. 'I can't believe this has happened. It's just typical of my luck. The day I was due to go off on leave last year, one of the helicopters suffered engine problems so the whole fleet was grounded. It played havoc with my plans, I can tell you.'

'Were you still able to take your holiday?' Seb asked.

'Yes, although by the time I'd re-booked the flight, I'd lost a couple of days. I was going to India, too, so it was a real drag.'

'Which part of India did you visit?' Seb asked sharply, glancing up.

'We were travelling around but we covered most of the west coast.'

'I see. That just might explain it.' He turned to Gary. 'Fetch me a bowl of cold water, will you?'

While Gary was sorting out the water, he picked up a wad of paper towels.

'What do you think it is?' Libby asked curiously as she helped him arrange the paper towels in a thick wad under the patient's foot.

'A Guinea worm.' Seb smiled when he saw the surprise on her face.

'Really? I would never have thought of that.'

'Neither would I if David hadn't told us about his holiday.' He turned to the younger man. 'India is one of the places where the infection is rife. You probably acquired it while you were there last year.'

'And it's taken all this time to show up?' David exclaimed in shock.

'Yes. You catch Guinea worm disease from drinking water that contains water-fleas, which carry the larvae,' he explained. 'The larvae pass through the wall of your intestine and mature in your body tissue. After about a year or so, the female worm—which is pregnant—approaches the surface of the skin and creates a blister.'

'You're saying there's a *worm* in there?' David demanded, looking sick.

'There's a simple way to find out.'

Seb took the basin of water off Gary and slowly poured it over the blister. Nothing happened for a couple of seconds then suddenly the blister broke, releasing a gush milky fluid, and the head of the worm appeared. Taking a pencil out of his pocket, he wound the worm around it.

'Just how long is that thing?' David asked shakily.

'About a metre, possibly a bit more.' He turned to Gary who was looking just as repulsed as the patient was. 'He'll need a course of thiabendazole to reduce the inflammation and make it easier to extract the worm.'

'How do we get it out?' Gary asked, recovering his composure.

'The time-honoured method is to wind the worm around a stick and ease it out a bit at a time.' He smiled when David grimaced. 'I know it sounds gross but it's the best way. Once it's out, we'll give you a tetanus booster and put you on antibiotics.'

'And that will be it? There won't be any more of the little suckers in there, will there?' David demanded. 'I don't want to wake up one morning and find there's another one!'

'Hopefully, this should be it, but I'll check with the tropical diseases centre in Liverpool to make sure. Our main aim now is to prevent any secondary infection of the worm track. Cellulitis—inflammation of the subcutaneous tissue—is fairly common in cases like this, plus it can also cause synovitis, which is inflammation in the membranes lining the joints. There is also a risk of epididymo-orchitis.'

'And what's that when it's at home?' David asked faintly.

'Inflammation of the testes,' Gary explained helpfully, and David gulped.

'That's all I need!'

Seb laughed. 'Don't worry too much on that score. We aim to stop any infection before it starts. The antibiotics should do the trick but make sure you take them regularly and finish the full course, won't you?'

'Too right I will.' David shuddered. 'So how long is it going to take before that thing is out?'

'That I can't tell you. I'll know more after I've spoken to the people at the tropical diseases unit, but I might not be able to get hold of them until later today.'

Seb nodded to Gary, indicating that he wanted a word with him outside. Libby stayed behind and he could hear her talking to the patient as they left the cubicle. She was obviously reassuring him than everything would be fine, and he sighed because it was typical of her to do that. She had such a tender heart and the thought made him feel worse than ever when he realised how hurt she must have been in the past year. Was it any wonder that she'd given up on him?

'We'll need someone to keep an eye on him,' he said briskly, trying not to dwell on that thought. 'I'm no expert, but from what I can remember, the worm can sometimes retreat into the body—and we don't want that to happen.'

'We certainly don't,' Gary agreed. 'Leave it with me, Seb—I'll sort it out. I'm just glad that you came up with the correct diagnosis because I would never have guessed what it was in a million years.'

'More luck than judgement,' Seb said lightly.

'Oh, I don't think so. Do you, Libby? Wouldn't you agree that it was a prime example of good diagnosis?'

'Yes. But Seb has always been brilliant at diagnosing a problem,' she said quietly as she came to join them. 'That's why he is so good at his job.'

Seb didn't know what to say. That she could be so generous as to praise him after what had happened was almost too much. 'Thanks, but it was no big deal.' He drummed up a laugh. 'And the next time you see a blister like that, you'll know what to expect.'

'Too right I will,' Gary said with a shudder. 'I won't forget this in a hurry.'

'That's the main thing.'

Seb moved away but his heart was heavy as he made his way to the office. Libby's generosity had simply highlighted how much they had changed in the last few years. In the past they had relished each other's successes, no matter how minor they'd been. They had been a team, both in and out of work. He realised all of a sudden how much he had missed working with her since she'd gone into general practice. He'd missed being able to talk over a problem with her, or even just share the everyday ups and downs that came with his job.

Was that when they had started to drift apart?

They'd no longer had the bond of work to unite them and they'd made the mistake of not replacing it with something else. As their working lives had diverged, so too had their relationship. He'd focussed so much energy on his career that he'd had little left to spare for her. How many times had she tried to tell him about her day, for instance, and he'd only half listened, too caught up in his own affairs to realise the harm he had been doing?

No wonder she no longer wanted him as her husband. He wasn't worthy of her love, and it was the bitterest thought of all to know that he had brought this on himself. If she gave him a second chance, he wouldn't make that mistake again. He would be there for her and cherish their life together. Maybe there was little hope of winning her back but he wouldn't give up until he had explored every avenue.

There *had* to be a way to persuade her to stay with him. All he had to do was find it before she left here. In his heart, he knew that there would never be another opportunity and the thought filled him with terror. It was now or never.

CHAPTER FOURTEEN

Saturday: 4 a.m.

'YOU should have seen it. It was absolutely gross!'

Everyone laughed as Gary finished telling them in glorious detail about the Guinea worm. They were in the rest room, taking advantage of the fact that there'd been a lull in the proceedings. Apart from a couple of patients who were waiting to move onto the wards, the department was empty. Libby hadn't been able to come up with an excuse when Gary had invited her to join them for a cup of coffee. Anyway, it had helped to pass the time, which was what she wanted more than anything. The sooner this night was over, the better.

She glanced across at Seb and felt her heart

contract when the reality of the situation struck her all over again. He didn't love her any more because he'd found someone to replace her. The thought was simply more than she could bear and she stood up abruptly, knowing that she had to leave the room before she made a fool of herself.

'You're not running out on us, are you, Libby?' Gary demanded when she went to the door.

'I just need a breath of fresh air,' she replied, dredging up a smile. Maybe it shouldn't have mattered what Seb did when they were about to get divorced, but she couldn't help how she felt. The thought of some other woman replacing her in his affections was just too painful.

'I wouldn't blame you if you were making a bid for freedom. You drove all the way up here expecting to spend some quality time with Seb, and what happens? You end up working!' Gary rolled his eyes. 'The truly amazing thing is that not once have you complained. My fiancée would have my guts for garters if I dared to suggest that she should help out. Obviously

I'm doing something wrong. I think I'd better ask Seb for a few tips on how to promote marital harmony before I risk walking up the aisle!'

The comment elicited a lot of ribald comments but Libby couldn't even pretend to find it amusing. She quickly excused herself and made her way to the main entrance, wishing that she could get into her car and drive away. However, she knew that she and Seb needed to finalise the arrangements for their divorce and that putting off the moment would only make the situation more stressful.

'Are you all right?'

She glanced round when she realised that Seb must have followed her outside. 'Fine. I just wanted a few minutes on my own,' she replied pointedly.

'In other words, you want me to get lost?' He laughed when she didn't deny it. 'I understand, Libby, but you were the one who drove all the way up here to see me, don't forget.'

'I haven't forgotten. However, what I want to say to you needs to be said in private.'

'Fair enough.' He shot back his cuff and checked his watch. 'It's just gone four so I'm hoping that things will start to wind down now. There's a debriefing session at six for the senior management team but I should be able to get away straight after that. Let's leave it until then, shall we? We can go back to my house and talk there.'

He sounded so calm, so reasonable, that a shiver ran through her. How could he behave this way when they were on the brink of such a momentous decision? Did he no longer care what happened any more?

Her heart ached because she sensed it was true. Seb seemed to have accepted now that their marriage had run its course. And the fact that he wasn't going to try and fight to keep her merely proved that she'd been right to ask him for a divorce.

'That sounds like the best idea to me,' she agreed, trying to match his businesslike manner. If the truth were told, he probably felt relieved that she had made the first move, in which case she wasn't going to let him know how heart-rending she found it to plan the demise of their marriage.

She lifted her chin and looked him in the eyes. 'I'll meet you here just after seven, shall I?'

'Please. The meeting shouldn't last very long. Everyone will be keen to go home so it should be more a formality than anything else. We'll do the in-depth assessment later. I should be through by seven-fifteen at the latest.'

'I'll see you then.'

Libby made her way across the forecourt after he'd gone back inside. It had stopped raining at last, although the wind was still very strong. She stopped when she reached the gates and turned to look back at the hospital. Now she had a time limit to work towards—three more hours to get through before she and Seb sat down and decided their future. Although she had gone over the scene in her mind a dozen times or more, she still couldn't imagine what would happen beyond that point. Obviously there would be various formalities to complete before their separation became legal, but after that—what? What kind of a life was she going to have without Seb?

Closing her eyes, she tried to picture it but the future was like a blank canvas: there was no colour, no shape, no form. Her life had revolved around him for so long that she couldn't envisage being without him. Even though they had been living apart for the past year, her first thought on waking each morning was about him, as was her last thought each night. Seb was the beginning and the end of her day, and that's how she'd always expected it would continue. She couldn't begin to guess how she was going to carry on without him.

'What's their ETA?'

Seb frowned as the operator explained that the air ambulance was due to land at the hospital in approximately ten minutes' time. It was bringing in two more men from the stricken tanker. Although the exact details weren't known yet, it was believed that they had been in contact with some of the chemicals.

He thanked the operator and hung up, mentally rehearsing what needed to be done before the helicopter arrived. This kind of situation could have far-reaching conse-quences for everyone concerned and there were protocols that would need to be followed. The men would have to be decontaminated before they were examined so that meant calling on the services of the local branch of the fire brigade. They would set up a decon-tamination unit in the hospital's grounds so that the seamen and the air ambulance's crew could be screened.

That wouldn't be the end of the matter, however. The fact that contamination had occurred meant that everyone still on board the tanker would need to be decontaminated as well, and then they would have to be checked over. It would definitely up the ante. Instead of winding down, they were going to have to gear themselves up for another influx of patients. Damn!

He got in touch with the local fire brigade then went back to the rest room and broke the news to his team. 'The air ambulance is on its way with two members of the tanker's crew who've been contaminated by a chemical spillage. Marilyn, I want you to do a preliminary assessment once they've been through decontamination. Gary, you can help her. We're going to have to screen everyone who's left onboard the tanker so I'd like Cathy, Grace and Ruth to process the men once they're ready to be seen. Jayne, I want you to go home. There's no point taking any risks when we don't know what we could be dealing with.'

Nobody questioned his instructions—they all understood the seriousness of the situation and the potential hazards involved. He left them to get ready and went to the storeroom. The Grace Darling Hospital played a key role in any major incidents in the area and they carried a wide range of equipment. Now he took a chemical hazard suit out of the cupboard and pulled it on over his clothes. There were built-in bootees to wear over his shoes, as well as gloves to protect his hands. There was also a hood and a breathing mask, although he wouldn't need to use them on this occasion.

He left the storeroom and almost ran right into Libby, who had been passing along the corridor. She looked at him in dismay when she realised what he was wearing.

'Does that mean what I think it does?'

'Chemical contamination,' he confirmed succinctly.

'How many casualties?'

'Two that we know about, but there could be more. We're going to have to screen everyone who leaves the tanker.'

'That could be dozens of people!' she exclaimed, and he sighed.

'It could, which means that I might not be finished by seven after all.'

'It doesn't matter,' she said quickly, so quickly, in fact, that he frowned. Bearing in mind that he'd just told her that their plans might have to be put on hold, she hadn't sounded upset by the idea. If anything, she'd seemed relieved and that didn't fit with the fact that she'd gone to all the trouble to drive up here to see him. He was just about to find out what was going on when she spoke.

'I'd like to help, if I can. I'm fully conversant with the new protocols for dealing with chemical contamination because I've just been on a course, so should I get kitted up?'

Seb hesitated for only a second, but he had to admit that he would be glad of her help now that Jayne had been sent home. 'Thanks. I appreciate the offer.'

He led the way back to the storeroom, keying in the security number to unlock the door. 'The protective suits are in this cupboard,' he explained, showing her where they were kept. 'Help yourself.'

She unhooked one of the suits and stepped into it, smiling wryly as she pulled it over her clothes. 'These things are so bulky, aren't they? I always feel like that cartoon character you used to see in those old adverts for car tyres whenever I have to wear one!'

'The Michelin man.' Seb laughed at the analogy. 'If it's any consolation, you don't look at all like him even in that get-up.'

'Thanks.' She zipped up the suit and grinned at him. 'Not that you would have dared to say so even if you had noticed a resemblance.'

'Too right I wouldn't.' He chuckled. 'I don't have a death wish, thank you very much!'

'Cheek! When have I ever taken offence if you've said you don't like what I'm wearing?' she demanded.

'Never. But that's because I've never criticised your choice of clothing.' He smiled at her. 'You always look lovely, Libby.'

'Oh, well, that's all right, then, isn't it?' she said, sounding rather flustered by the compliment.

She hurried to the door and Seb quickly followed her, wondering if this might be a good time to try and win her round. He needed to tell her that he cared about her and hopefully that would pave the way towards the rest.

'Look, Libby,' he began, then stopped when the sound of rotors overhead announced that the air ambulance had arrived. 'That sounds like the helicopter,' he said, bitterly aware that he had missed his chance. All he could do was hope that there would be another opportunity later, but it was scary to know that time was passing and that he still hadn't done anything to resolve the situation.

'We'd better go and meet them,' Libby said, opening the door.

They made their way straight up to the roof but the helicopter had already landed by the time they got there. Seb knew that he had to put everything else out of his mind while he focussed on what needed doing. The paramedics grinned when they saw what he and Libby were wearing, but he knew they must be worried about the effects it could have on them if they'd been contaminated by the chemicals.

'OK, guys, I know we look like something out of one of those old disaster movies but we can't afford to take any chances. I want you lot downstairs in the decontamination unit PDQ.'

There was a bit of half-hearted muttering about it being a waste of time but they soon complied with his instructions. In a very short space of time the paramedics and the seamen from the tanker were lining up outside the mobile decontamination unit. The fire brigade had performed the procedure many times before so it didn't take long: each man was told to strip and then walk through a series of showers which removed all traces of the chemicals from his skin.

The seamen's clothes were bagged and would need to be burned so regulation hospital gowns were handed out to them. The air ambulance crew fared slightly better—their clothing was designed for use in areas where there might be chemical contamination so it would be cleaned and returned to them. In the meantime, they were provided with cotton scrubs and sent inside to be checked over.

By the time Seb and Libby had removed their protective clothing, Marilyn had taken the seamen into the end two cubicles. The curtains had been drawn to form one large examination area so there was room for all of them in there.

'How do they look?' Seb asked as soon as they went in.

'Not too bad, considering.' Marilyn nodded to one of the men. 'Dimitri has superficial burns on his hands. They should heal well enough so we don't need to call in the burns registrar. It's his legs I'm more concerned about. Apparently, when the container split open, a lot of the chemical spilled over his legs and feet.'

'Do we know exactly what it is yet?' Libby asked, bending down to examine the man's legs.

Seb crouched down beside her but there was little visible sign that the seaman had come into contact with any hazardous material, apart from a slight redness to his skin. Sadly, it wasn't an indication that no harm had been done, though. Persistent organic pollutants—POPs—were highly toxic and had the potential to damage human health even at very low concentrations. Some POPs were also hormone disruptors and interfered with the natural production of hormones in a person's body so their effects could be far-reaching. There was no way of knowing how badly they would affect this man in the future.

'The owners are being very evasive,' Marilyn explained dryly. 'Hopefully, we'll know more once we get a sample of the chemicals tested when the tanker is brought into port.'

'*If* it's brought into port, you mean,' Seb amended, standing up. 'There's no knowing what's going to happen to it in this weather.'

Libby sighed as she stood up as well. 'We'll just have to keep our fingers *and* our toes crossed, won't we?'

Seb nodded, although he hated feeling as though he was working in the dark. He much preferred it when he was in possession of all the facts—that way he knew exactly what to do, although it didn't apply to his marriage, did it? He knew exactly what was going to happen and he still had no idea what he was going to do about it.

He glanced at the clock and felt his heart accelerate when he realised that it was already one minute before five. There were just a couple more hours to go before he and Libby were due to leave the hospital and it wasn't long enough. He needed more time to come up with a plan. He couldn't afford to rush and risk making any more mistakes…

The clock ticked as the minute hand complete its circuit of the dial. Seb groaned. Five a.m. He'd just wasted another precious minute!

CHAPTER FIFTEEN

Saturday: 5 a.m.

LIBBY glanced at the clock as they left the cubicle and was surprised to discover that it was 5 a.m. already. The time seemed to be flying past now and she couldn't help feeling nervous at the thought of what was going to happen in a couple of hours' time.

She sighed. Not that long ago she could hardly wait for the moment when she would be able to talk to Seb about their divorce, yet now she found herself wishing that she could delay it, and she simply couldn't afford to start having doubts at this stage. She had to stick to the decision she'd made, no matter how difficult it was.

'I'd better check with the incident control centre. We need some idea of how many more casualties we can expect.' Seb paused as they came to the end of the corridor.

'There can't be that many more, surely,' Libby said, frowning.

'I hope not, but you never know, do you?' He gave her a quick, almost abstracted smile. 'I'll catch up with you later. OK?'

'Fine.'

Libby headed towards Reception. She knew there must be other people waiting to be seen so she would see if she could help speed up the process. Cathy was just coming out of the treatment room as she passed so Libby stopped.

'Is there anything I can do to help?'

'Not really. We've got everything covered, thank you.'

Cathy's tone was cool and Libby frowned. The nurse had been very offhand with her ever since she'd arrived and she had no idea what she'd done to upset her...unless Cathy was the woman whom Seb had been seeing. After all, nothing brought two people closer than a shared interest in their work, and Cathy was ideally placed to be Seb's sounding board. The idea of the nurse sharing all the highs and lows of his job with him hurt unbearably and she went to walk on, but Cathy stopped her.

'Why did you come here tonight, Libby?'

'I came to see Seb, of course,' she replied, unsure where the question was leading.

'But why tonight, though?' Cathy shrugged when Libby looked at her in confusion. 'I mean, it's not as though you've bothered making the effort very often before. It must be months since you were last up here.'

'It isn't always easy to get away,' Libby said tightly, resenting the implied criticism. 'We held a Saturday morning surgery at the practice where I work up until a few of months ago. I couldn't just disappear for the weekend whenever I chose to do so.'

'Most GPs use a rota system to work out their weekends,' Cathy pointed out. 'I can't imagine that you had to work every single weekend, did you?'

'No, I didn't. But neither does Seb, for that matter,' she said crisply, refusing to accept all the blame for their lack of contact.

'Seb works more weekends than he has off. It's become a standing joke around here that if you need a consultant over the weekend, you phone the trauma unit. More often than not, Seb's somewhere around, which is sad when you think about it. He should have more to do with his weekends than hang around here, don't you think?'

Libby had no idea what to say in reply. She was just too surprised to learn that Seb had been spending his weekends working. If that was true, could he have found the time to carry on an affair with Cathy—or anyone else, for that matter? She was still floundering around for something to say when Seb himself appeared.

'Sorry to interrupt, ladies, but I've just found out that the rest of the crew from the tanker are being ferried here. Cathy, can you make sure that everyone goes through the decontamination process before they enter the building? I don't want any mix-ups.'

'Of course.'

Cathy gave him a warm smile and hurried

away, leaving Libby feeling more confused than ever. There was no doubt in her mind that the nurse thought very highly of Seb, but was she involved with him on a personal level as well as a professional one? All of a sudden she knew that she had to find out the answer before it drove her crazy.

'You seem to have a really good rapport with your team,' she said hurriedly before he could leave. 'Do you see much of them out of work as well as in?'

'Sometimes.' He shrugged, although she could tell that he was a little puzzled by the question. 'It's just the usual sort of socialising—trips to the pub, the odd meal out, that sort of thing.'

'Does Cathy go with you?' she asked, trying to make it appear that the question had been prompted by mild curiosity.

'If she gets the chance, yes, she does. But more often than not she's in a rush to get home.' Seb folded his arms and regarded her steadily. 'She has five-year-old twin boys so her free time is pretty limited, as you might imagine.'

'Oh, I see.'

Libby looked away when she felt embarrassed colour sweep up her face. It seemed that she'd been wrong to assume that Cathy was the woman Seb had been seeing, although it didn't mean that he wasn't involved with someone else. She looked up when she heard him sigh heavily.

'I am not having an affair with Cathy. From what I know, she is very happily married, although nobody really knows what goes on in someone else's marriage, do they?'

Libby flinched when she heard the bitterness in his voice. However, before she could say anything, Marilyn appeared. 'Sorry, Seb, but you're needed. One of the guys they've just brought in has collapsed. It doesn't look too promising either.'

'I'll be right there.' He turned to her and Libby could see the reproach in his eyes. 'I know how hard it is, but try not to let your imagination run away with you. The situation isn't what you think it is.'

She wasn't sure what he meant by that but as

she watched him hurry across the waiting room, she could feel her heart racing. Had Seb been trying to tell her that there was no other woman in his life?

She wanted to believe it was true but if it was, why hadn't he told her so before? Why hadn't he denied that he'd been having an affair when she'd accused him earlier on?

'He needs intubating. Can someone shine a light over here so I can see what the hell I'm doing?'

Seb could hear the snap in his voice but he refused to apologise for it. He was sick and tired of being made to feel as though he had done something wrong when he wasn't to blame!

He picked up the laryngoscope, nodding when a light appeared over his right shoulder. He mustn't think about Libby and this crazy idea she'd got into her head about him having an affair or he wouldn't be able to do his job properly. 'Shine that light a bit more to the left,' he instructed, determined to get a grip on himself. 'OK, hold it right there.'

He carefully passed the endotracheal tube

down the patient's throat between his vocal cords into his trachea. Removing the laryngoscope, he taped the end of the tube into place then glanced at Marilyn. 'Right. Bag him.'

He stood up as the registrar attached the end of the breathing bag to the tube and began to rhythmically pump oxygen into the patient's lungs. The man had collapsed before they had managed to get him into the decontamination unit so they were working outside on the forecourt. It wasn't the ideal spot to resuscitate a patient, but beggars couldn't be choosers. And in this instance, there was a lot to be said for keeping him outside. He glanced round when Ruth asked him if she should fetch a trolley so they could move him.

'Not yet. I'd really like to get him through the decontamination process before we do anything else. Let's give him a couple of minutes and see how things go from there.'

He knelt down again as Marilyn continued to pump oxygen into the man's lungs. 'How was he on the way here?' he asked, glancing up at a member of the ambulance crew.

'He didn't seem any worse than the other guys.' The paramedic shrugged. 'They were all very quiet on the way in—probably in shock after everything they've been through tonight.'

'Did they mention that they'd been in contact with any chemicals?' Seb queried, checking the man's pulse and frowning when he realised how thready it was.

'No. They said very little. I just assumed they didn't speak much English.' The paramedic glanced round when someone shouted his name. 'Looks like it's my turn for the showers. Sorry I can't be of more help, Doc.'

'Don't apologise. It's not your fault he's in this state,' Seb assured him.

He turned his attention back to the patient. He had already established that there were no major injuries, but the man's breathing was definitely compromised. In the absence of any other information, he could only assume it was the result of coming into contact with the chemicals that had been transported on board the tanker. Even commonly used organophosphate pesticides, which could be bought in the local garden centre, could cause irreversible damage by binding to an essential brain enzyme called AchE, and the chemicals transported on board the tanker were far more dangerous than that. It was impossible to quantify the effect they might have had so it was a case of supporting the patient until he recovered sufficiently to tell them what had happened, and that could take some time.

Seb came to swift decision, knowing he couldn't keep the man outside indefinitely. 'We'll move him into the isolation suite. We need to get those clothes off him and make sure any chemical residue is washed off. I'd prefer to do it myself than risk anyone else getting contaminated.'

'Come on, Seb, there's no need for that,' Marilyn protested. 'So long as we take the proper precautions, there's no reason why one of us can't help you.'

'I'd really rather that you didn't,' he said firmly. 'You know as well as I do the long-term effect POPs can have, and I can't see any sense in you taking risks with your health.'

'I can't see any sense in you taking them either,' Marilyn said stoutly. 'You don't want to ruin your chances of becoming a dad, do you?'

'There's no chance of that happening.'

Seb turned away, afraid that his expression would be far too revealing. Hopefully, Marilyn would take his comment at face value and assume that he was denying there was a risk to his fertility. However, there had been more to it than that.

There was no chance of him becoming a father now that Libby was going to divorce him, and the thought was the bitterest of all the blows he'd suffered that night. To know that he might never have the family he'd dreamed of made him want to howl in despair, only men weren't supposed to cry about things like that. They were supposed to shrug and get on with their lives, and maybe he should do that too, but he simply couldn't handle the thought that he and Libby would never have a child together, that he would never get the chance to cradle their son or daughter in his arms. Tears welled to his eyes and he was glad of the poor lighting because at least it spared him the embarrassment of everyone seeing how devastated he felt. 'I'll get everything set up,' he said gruffly, turning away.

He went inside and told Cathy what was happening then left her to get the isolation room ready while he spoke to the hospital's chief executive and brought him up to speed. The CEO wasn't pleased at the thought of there being a possible contamination issue inside the building so it took a few minutes of intense discussion plus some thinly veiled threats about what the press would make of the story if they got hold of it before he agreed, but Seb didn't care. It was the right thing to do and, by heaven, he was going to see it through to the end!

He collected a trolley and went back outside. One of the paramedics offered to help him so between them they lifted the man onto the trolley and took him to the isolation room. Seb donned a double layer of gloves then set about removing the patient's clothing and bagging it.

There was a huge patch of some kind of chemical residue all down his chest and abdomen so Seb washed it off then summoned Cathy and asked her to attach the man to the monitoring equipment. She'd just finished when he arrested.

Seb hit the crash button. 'I'll give him a shot of adrenaline,' he said as Cathy began cardiac massage. The rest of the team arrived at a run and took up their positions. Libby was with them and he couldn't help his heart sinking when he saw her. His emotions were too raw, too near to the surface at the moment, but he could hardly order her to leave.

'Can you trade places with Cathy?' he instructed, stamping hard on his feelings.

'Of course.'

She stepped up to the bed and took over from the nurse, quickly settling into a rhythm as she carried out the vital chest compressions that were keeping the patient's blood circulating around his system. Seb drew up the drug and swiftly administered it, but there was still no output.

'Asystole,' Marilyn confirmed from across the bed.

'We'll try defibrillating him.' He lifted the paddles and rubbed them with a little gel while Marilyn set the machine. 'Clear!' he snapped, then watched as the patient's whole body jerked when the electric current passed through him.

'Sinus rhythm,' Marilyn announced, and everyone breathed a sigh of relief.

'I want him on an intravenous infusion of sodium bicarbonate,' Seb instructed, even though it was normal practice to administer it in all cases of cardiac arrest. When the heart stopped, the chemical balance of the blood was altered too, making it more acidic. Sodium bicarbonate was given to correct the balance as a matter of course, but he never left anything to chance. 'I also want him on lignocaine to stabilise the heart muscle. We don't want to have to go through this all over again.'

By the time Seb left the isolation room some ten minutes later, the seaman was stable. He headed straight for the showers and stripped off his clothes. Although he had taken all the necessary precautions, it would be foolish not to make sure that he'd washed off every trace of those chemicals.

He stepped into a stall and turned the water to its hottest setting. Maybe he and Libby would never have that family they'd once dreamed about, but he might meet someone else one day, another woman he could love enough to have his child. He tried to picture her—this unknown woman—but his mind refused to obey him. The only image it would conjure up was one of Libby on their wedding day. She was smiling up at him, her beautiful face alight with happiness…

Closing his eyes, Seb let himself savour the moment all over again, and if his tears flowed then at least nobody saw them. They were washed away along with all the dreams he'd had for the future. Maybe he could win Libby back—he really didn't know. But could they ever get back what they'd felt on their wedding day, when each had been the centre of the other's world?

CHAPTER SIXTEEN

Saturday: 6 a.m.

'IS THERE anything else I can do?'

Libby was feeling at a bit of a loss when she spotted Seb coming out of the changing room. The rest of the crew from the tanker had been through the decontamination process now and were currently waiting to be examined. With Gary and Marilyn on hand to deal with them, she wasn't needed any more and she would have appreciated having something to do to help pass the last hour. Her stomach lurched at the thought of what was going to happen in an hour's time so that it was hard not to show how nervous she felt as Seb came over to her.

'I'm not sure what needs doing now. Why

don't you make yourself a cup of coffee? I'll give you a shout if I need you again.'

'Fine. I'll be in the rest room, then,' she said shortly, wondering if he'd set out to make her feel as though she was more of a hindrance than a help. She sighed as she made her way to the rest room because she was just being ridiculous now, imagining insults where none had been intended. Seb had more important things to do than play silly games with her!

She filled the kettle then realised that the others might be glad of a drink as well. It had been frantically busy for the past hour so there'd been no time to stop for a break. She left the rest room and was on her way to the cubicles when a woman accosted her.

'Excuse me, are you a doctor?'

'I am, although I'm not a member of the hospital's staff,' Libby explained.

'Oh, I see.' The young woman looked close to tears. 'Someone left a message on my answering machine to say my husband was here, and I need to find out what's happened to him.'

'If you can tell me his name, I'll see what I can find out for you,' Libby said gently.

'It's Alistair…Alistair Roberts. He's a pilot with the air-sea rescue team.'

Libby's heart sank because Alistair was the man she had found with the metal spike through his side. Although he'd been sent to Theatre, she knew that the prognosis hadn't been good.

'I know who you mean,' she said carefully. 'I happened to be in the area when his helicopter crashed and I helped bring him in.'

'He *crashed*!'

The colour drained from the young woman's face and she swayed. Libby cursed herself for being so thoughtless as to assume that Alistair's wife had been told all the facts. Putting a hand under the poor woman's arm, she helped her to a chair then sat down beside her.

'I am *so* sorry. I just assumed you knew what had happened or I would never have told you that,' she explained regretfully, but the woman waved away her apology.

'It doesn't matter—really it doesn't. I just

want to know how Alistair is.' Her voice caught. 'We had a massive row this morning before I left for work, and I told him that I never wanted to see him again…'

She broke off in distress. Libby patted her arm, wishing there was something she could say to help. 'Try not to think about that now. It really isn't important.'

'You're right. It was just a stupid argument, too…the sort of thing that blows up out of nothing really.' She blew her nose, making an effort to collect herself. 'Alistair was annoyed because I'd agreed to work this weekend, you see. We've been saving up and I thought if I did an extra shift, the money would come in very useful, but he wanted us to spend some time together.'

'It's difficult to find the time to see each other when you're both working,' Libby said softly, trying not to think about her and Seb.

'It is. There just aren't enough hours in the day, especially when you do the kind of jobs Alistair and I do. I'm a flight attendant and I usually work on long-haul trips so I can be away for days at a time. With the kind of hours Ali works, not to mention the fact that he's often on call, we're rarely at home together.' She managed a watery smile. 'We're trying to get the house sorted out because we want to have a baby, although the odds on us being under the same roof long enough to make it happen aren't that great!'

'It's very difficult,' Libby murmured, trying not to let Mrs Roberts see that she had struck an all-too-familiar chord. She and Seb had never seemed to find the time to start that family they'd planned, and now it was never going to happen.

'It is, but never mind all that—tell me about Alistair. How badly injured is he? You said that you'd helped to bring him in so you must have seen him.'

'I did, and I'm afraid your husband was very badly injured, Mrs Roberts,' she explained gently. 'He was thrown from the helicopter when it crashed and impaled on a metal spike, which caused severe internal damage.'

'Oh!' The woman went whiter than ever as

she pressed her hand to her mouth. 'Did they get it out—the metal spike, I mean?'

'I haven't seen him since he was sent to Theatre so I'm afraid I can't tell you what's happened in the past few hours.' Libby patted her hand then stood up. 'If you would stay here, I'll see what I can find out for you.'

She left the woman in the waiting area and went to find Cathy, hoping the staff nurse would be able to tell her how she could find out about the pilot. Cathy pulled a face when she explained what she wanted.

'It didn't sound too hopeful when we sent him to Theatre but you can give the theatre admissions nurse a call to see how they got on. Here's her number. If he's been moved onto a ward, she'll be able to give you all the details.'

Libby thanked her and went to the phone. It was a few minutes before anyone answered and the news wasn't good: Alistair Roberts had died on the operating table.

She hung up, wondering how she was going to tell his wife what had happened. This was the part of the job she'd hated most of all when she'd worked in emergency care. No matter how many times she'd had to break bad news to a relative, it had never got any easier. She knew how devastated the poor woman was going to be because she could imagine how she would feel if she and Seb had had a row and something awful had happened to him…

A sob suddenly rose into her throat. Maybe it was a combination of stress and exhaustion, but she couldn't seem to control her emotions any more. Spinning round, she hurried back along the corridor, knowing that she couldn't let Mrs Roberts see her in this state. She was supposed to be a professional and know how to deal with situations like this, but it was just too much for her right now.

Tears streamed down her face as she bypassed the cubicles. She didn't even see Seb until she almost ran right into him. He grabbed hold of her arms and she could see the concern in his eyes when he saw the state she was in, but there was nothing she could do about it. If anything happened to him, she wouldn't want to carry on living!

'Libby, what is it? Tell me what's happened?'

Seb could feel his heart thundering with fright. He had no idea what had gone on but that mattered less than the fact that Libby…his *darling* Libby…was sobbing her heart out.

He pulled her into his arms and held her as sobs racked her, knowing that he would have cut off his right arm if it would have helped. He would do anything in his power to keep her safe and make her happy, walk over hot coals, fight dragons, give up his career—anything at all. He was finally beginning to understand that nothing in the world had ever mattered to him as much as she did, and nothing ever would.

'Sh, it's all right. I'm here and I've got you,' he murmured. If he had realized that fact before, they wouldn't have drifted apart and certainly wouldn't be heading for the divorce courts. If he had faced the fact that his life revolved around her, they would still be together!

The thought of how stupid he'd been was more than he could bear, but his feelings had to come second to hers. Tilting her chin, he looked at her tear-stained face and sighed. 'Tell me what's happened. Maybe there's something I can do about it.'

'I don't think you can…'

Another sob racked her but he didn't try to rush her. If she needed time to tell him, he would give it to her, and give her anything else if it would help. She only had to ask and he would be there for her, ready and more than willing, but would she ask him for help now?

At one point, she had come to him whenever she'd had a problem, but the further apart they'd grown, the less frequently it had happened. He couldn't remember the last time that she had asked him for anything and it was painful to know that it was his own fault.

He hadn't been there for her when she'd needed him, but he would be there for her now and in the future if she would let him. If she was willing to try again, he swore on his life that he would never let her down again. Maybe they couldn't recapture the magic of their wedding day but he could be happy with less so long as she trusted him.

Did she?
Could she?
Would she?
Seb held his breath.

CHAPTER SEVENTEEN

Saturday: 7 a.m.

'ALISTAIR ROBERTS'S wife has just arrived—you remember the pilot of that helicopter which crashed last night... Or was it this morning?'

Libby frowned as she tried to recall exactly when the crash had happened, but so much had gone on since then, it was impossible to remember.

'I know who you mean.'

'Of course you do.' She dredged up a smile, although there was something about the way Seb was looking at her now which made her feel very on edge. She had the strangest feeling that he was hanging onto her every word, although she had no idea why.

'Cathy told me to phone Theatre to see if they could tell me how he'd got on,' she explained, before she got sidetracked. Her voice caught again. 'H-he died during surgery, apparently.'

'He was very badly injured,' Seb said quietly. 'The odds were stacked against him from the outset, Libby.'

'I know, but it's going to hit his wife really hard.' She took a tissue out of her pocket and dried her eyes. Seb dealt with death on a daily basis and she didn't want him to think that she was overreacting.

'Of course it will hit her hard. It's bound to have had an effect on you, too, because you were involved in trying to save his life.' He squeezed her hand. 'Don't feel bad because you're upset. It just shows that you care and that isn't something to be ashamed of.'

'I thought you'd think I was being silly,' she admitted. She shrugged when he looked at her in surprise. 'I *am* a doctor and I'm supposed to be able to behave in a professional manner when someone dies.'

'Maybe. But that doesn't mean that you aren't affected when something like this happens. We all are. It's only too easy to imagine how we'd feel if the same thing happened to us.'

'That's what got to me most of all. I kept thinking how I would feel if I was in that poor woman's shoes—'

She broke off abruptly. It was hardly the right moment to admit how devastated she would feel if anything happened to him. She cleared her throat. 'I'll have to go back and tell her what's happened to her husband.'

'Do you want me to do it? I'm the one who dealt with him when he was admitted so it's my responsibility to speak to his relatives, not yours.'

'It's kind of you to offer, Seb, but it would be better if I did it.' She sighed. 'Remember what they used to tell us when we were students? Maintaining personal contact with a relative makes it easier for them. It's doubly stressful for them when bad news is given to them by a total stranger.'

'I know all that but I don't want you getting yourself upset over this.' He gripped her hand. 'It's been a tough night, Libby, for many reasons, and there's no point piling on the pressure when you don't have to. I will tell Alistair's wife if it will make it easier for you.'

'Thanks. I really appreciate the offer but it's up to me to do it.'

She gently withdrew her hand, more touched than she dared to admit by his thoughtfulness. She'd missed having him there to lean on in the past year but she had to get used to standing on her own two feet because Seb wasn't going to be around in the future to help her.

Her emotions were far too raw to handle that thought so she quickly excused herself and made her way to Reception. Alistair's wife jumped to her feet as soon as Libby appeared.

'How is he? Do you know where they've taken him?'

'Let's sit down for a moment.' Libby eased her back down onto the chair then took hold of her hand, struggling to keep her own emotions in check. 'I am so very sorry to have to tell you this, but the surgeons weren't able to save your husband. Alistair died while he was in Theatre.'

'Died? No, that can't be right! It must be a mistake. They must have got him mixed up with someone else!' Mrs Roberts leapt to her feet and looked frantically around the waiting room. 'I need to find out where he is and sort this out…'

'It isn't a mistake. I am so very sorry but Alistair was too badly injured and he didn't survive the operation.' Libby stood up and put her arm around the woman's shoulders. 'Is there someone I can call for you? A friend or a relative who could be with you?'

'I don't know… I can't seem to think straight.' The woman's eyes were glazed with shock as she looked beseechingly at Libby. 'Can I see him? I need to actually see him before I can believe it's true.'

'Of course you can see him. I'll take you to him right away and you can sit with him for as long as you want to.'

Libby could feel her emotions welling up again as she led the woman to the lift. It took every scrap of self-control she could muster not to give in to them. She escorted Alistair's wife to the mortuary and waited while she saw her husband and said her goodbyes. Maybe it wasn't really her job but she couldn't just abandon the poor woman.

The poor soul was devastated when they left so Libby took her to the relatives' room and sat with her until she had calmed down enough to go home. She phoned for a taxi to take her because it wasn't safe for Mrs Roberts to drive in that state. By the time the cab arrived, it was almost eight o'clock—way past the time she'd arranged to meet Seb.

She collected her belongings and went to the main door, but there was no sign of him when she got there. He must have been detained at his meeting so she would have to wait until he was ready to leave.

If she was honest, she was glad of the delay. She still felt as though she needed more time before she had to face the biggest ordeal of her life. Although Seb seemed to have accepted what was about to happen, she knew that it wasn't going to be easy for either of them. They were bound to have regrets, but what could she do? If he didn't love her any more, it would be far better if they went their separate ways.

Seb glanced impatiently at his watch. The meeting had run on far longer than he'd expected it to. The main sticking point seemed to be the disappearance of the missing seaman. Despite an extensive search of the hospital and its grounds, the police had been unable to find him. He shook his head when someone suggested that the staff who had been working during the night should be interviewed before they left in case they could shed any light on the man's whereabouts.

'It would be a complete waste of time, in my opinion. We dealt with dozens of people last night, and we were far too busy to keep track of one man's comings and goings.'

He pushed back his chair, knowing that if he didn't make a move, the meeting would drag on. Most of the people there had been tucked up in their beds last night instead of working.

'I'm sorry, but I'm going to call it a day. I'll be back in this afternoon if there are any further questions, but that's it for now.'

Some of the board members looked less than impressed but he didn't care. He had been on the go since eight o'clock the previous day and he was exhausted. He made his way downstairs and checked that his team was ready to leave. Those members of staff who hadn't been called in during the night would take over while everyone else went home. However, before they left, he wanted to thank them.

'I want to thank you all for what you did last night. It was a real team effort and we should be proud of ourselves for what we achieved.' He turned to Gary. 'What was the final tally?'

'One hundred and three,' the registrar announced, grinning.

'Which means I owe you a fiver, junior.' Marilyn handed over a five-pound note. 'Don't spend it all on sweeties or you'll ruin your teeth.'

'Yes, Mum.' Gary smirked as he pocketed the money. 'Now, admit it—I don't exaggerate the size of everything, do I?'

'I don't know about that,' Marilyn retorted. 'I'll have to check with your girlfriend before I can answer that question.'

Everyone laughed, and Seb shook his head. 'You two are incorrigible. Right, that's it, folks. Off you go home to your beds. I'll see you all back here whenever.'

There was a spontaneous round of applause before everyone started to disperse. Seb was too tired to go upstairs to his office to fetch his jacket so he didn't bother. He had his car keys and his house keys in his pocket so he would leave his jacket here and collect it when he came back that afternoon. He made his way to the exit, breathing in deeply as he stepped outside into the morning air. The wind had dropped now and the day had that washed-clean feel about it which often followed a storm. If it weren't for the fact that he still had to get through this meeting with Libby, he would have described it as a glorious day, but knowing what was to come took all the pleasure out of it.

This might be the last time they would be

together as husband and wife if he didn't do something to stop what was happening. Maybe Libby hadn't taken him up on his offer to help her before, but he couldn't afford to let that influence him. He had to make her understand that they still had a lot to give one another. It wasn't a lie. He needed her as much now as he'd done when they had married!

He took a deep breath as panic gripped him. He still didn't know how he was going to accomplish his mission, but somehow he had to convince her to give him and their marriage a second chance.

CHAPTER EIGHTEEN

Saturday: 8 a.m.

'SORRY to keep you waiting. The meeting ran on longer than I expected it to.'

Libby looked up when Seb approached the bench where she was sitting. 'It doesn't matter. I was glad of a breather. It was a busy night, wasn't it?' she added hurriedly, because she didn't want him making too much of that comment.

'It certainly was.'

He gave her a noncommittal smile and her heart sank because she knew that he was deliberately distancing himself from her. She tried not to let him see how much it hurt to be treated that way as she followed him to the car park. She had no right to complain in view of the reason why she had come to see him, but she would have felt so much better if he had treated her the way he normally did—warmly, kindly and with love.

Tears stung her eyes when she realised how stupid it was to expect that of him now. When he stopped beside his car, she made a conscious effort to disguise her feelings. The only way she was going to get through this was by keeping her emotions under wraps.

'Shall we go in my car?' he suggested, opening the door.

'It would be easier if I took my own car.' She shrugged. 'That way, you won't need to drive me back here afterwards, will you?'

'Of course not.'

He didn't try to persuade her to travel with him and her heart sank even more. It was obvious that he'd accepted that she would be going back to Sussex after their talk and had no intention of trying to change her mind.

'I suggest you follow me, then. You've not been to the new house yet and it can be a bit tricky to find it if you don't know the way.' He got into the car and rolled down the window. 'I know it's Saturday but the traffic can be quite heavy in the centre of town so if we get separated, don't panic—I'll pull in and wait for you to catch up.'

'Thanks.'

Libby hurried over to her car. She backed out of the space and drove round to where Seb was waiting for her. He gave her a quick wave then headed towards the exit, turning right as soon as they left the hospital. As he'd predicted, the traffic was heavy and the town centre was virtually gridlocked. She groaned when they reached a junction and the traffic lights changed before she could follow him across the road. She had no idea where she was and could only hope that he would notice that she wasn't behind him.

It seemed to take for ever before the lights changed again. She crossed the junction and breathed a sigh of relief when she spotted him waiting by the kerb for her. She flashed her lights and they set off again, leaving the town behind after a couple of miles. The roads were quieter now and Seb picked up speed, although he didn't drive as fast as he would have done if she hadn't been following him. She'd always been a more cautious driver than he was and obviously he was making allowances for that.

Tears prickled her eyes again at the thought but she mustn't cry now. There would be plenty of time for tears when she was back in Sussex.

On her own.

Seb could feel his tension mounting the closer they got to the house. He kept desperately trying to think of a way to delay the inevitable but his mind just wouldn't function properly. All he could think about was that each mile he drove brought the moment when he would lose Libby that bit closer, and he didn't know how he was going to cope. Maybe he should just throw himself on her mercy and beg her not to leave him? He didn't care if he would be making a fool of himself. Anything had to be better than living out the rest of his days without her!

They came to the final bend in the road and there, straight ahead, was the house. As soon as he'd seen the photograph in the estate agent's window he'd known he had to buy it. Built at the beginning of the previous century, it stood on the side of a hill and offered spectacular views over the North Sea. Libby had always dreamed of living near the coast and he'd known that she would love it. It didn't matter if the windows needed replacing and the interior needed redecorating because she would see past all that. He had bought it in the hope that it might tempt her to move north, but now he could see how stupid he'd been. It would take more than bricks and mortar and wonderful views to mend their marriage!

Libby parked her car and switched off the engine. She wasn't sure what she'd been expecting but it hadn't been this. She got out of the car and stood for a moment, just drinking in the view. Pale, pearly grey light shimmered over the sea, turning the waves to liquid crystal, and her breath caught in awe at the sight.

'It doesn't matter what the weather is like because the view is always stunning.'

She turned as Seb came to stand beside her. 'You never told me the house was on the coast.'

'No. I was saving it as a surprise.' He gave her a quick smile but she saw the pain that had darkened his eyes before he turned away and realised that he was finding this every bit as difficult as she was.

She followed him up the path and waited in silence while he unlocked the front door, because there was nothing she could say to make this easier for either of them. He pushed the door wide open then stepped back.

'It's a bit shabby, I'm afraid. The previous owners lived here for almost fifty years so everything needs updating. I'll get round to it eventually, if I don't decide to sell it, of course.'

'Sell it!' she exclaimed, stepping into the hall. There was parquet flooring and a sweeping oak staircase leading to the upper floor. A stained-glass window on the landing spilled rainbow-coloured light along the dusty banister rail. It was the kind of house she'd always dreamed of owning and she couldn't imagine why he would consider selling it…

'It's too big for one person. It really needs a family to bring it back to life.' He closed the door and the quiet thud of the lock sounded so final that she could have wept.

'Maybe you'll meet someone else,' she suggested in a tight little voice.

'That seems highly unlikely at the moment.'

His face was set as he made for a door at the far side of the hall, and she had to stop herself running after him and flinging her arms around him. She knew that he was hurting but what could she do? If she changed her mind about the divorce, they would be right back where they'd started: he would be living up here and she would be living in Sussex and she couldn't bear this half-marriage they'd had for the past year. She wanted all or nothing, not a compromise. She wanted to be with him every day of the year or not be with him at all. Living the way they had been doing was tearing her apart!

Seb could feel tears welling up as he went into the kitchen. That Libby could even suggest that he would find someone to replace her just proved how futile it was to hope to win her back. Already she had moved on to the next stage, mentally if not physically…although there was no guarantee about that either, was there?

His blood seemed to turn to ice as he was forced to face the fact that she might have met someone else, someone she loved more than him.

He couldn't believe that he hadn't considered the idea before. After all, she was a beautiful and intelligent woman and there would be many men eager to spend their lives with her. Just because she'd been faithful to him in the past, it didn't mean that she had continued to be so, did it?

She had needs like any other woman had. She had dreams, too, of a family and a husband who put her and their children first. Had some other man stepped into her life while he'd been miles away at the other end of the country? Had she found in him all the things *he* hadn't been able to give her lately: security, comfort, love?

Seb could hardly bear to contemplate the idea

that Libby might have found someone else and that was why she had driven all this way to ask him for a divorce. Now he had a choice—either he could agree to divorce her and let her get on with her life, or he could make it difficult and stop her finding happiness with someone else.

Whatever he decided, one of them was going to get hurt. The only question now was could he live with himself if it was Libby?

CHAPTER NINETEEN

Saturday: 9 a.m.

'SEB…are you OK?'

Libby frowned when her husband failed to answer the question. Hurrying into the kitchen, she put her hand on his arm and felt him flinch.

'I'm fine. Just a bit spaced out after last night, I expect.' He stepped away from her and picked up the kettle. 'I don't know about you but I could do with a cup of coffee.'

'I…um…yes. Coffee would be great. Thanks.'

Libby dredged up a smile but she could tell that something had happened, though she had no idea what it could be. Pulling out a chair, she sat down at the table while he busied himself with the coffee.

'Fancy a bacon sandwich as well? I'm starving.'

He opened the door of the old-fashioned refrigerator and hunted around inside until he unearthed a packet of bacon, but Libby shook her head.

'No. I'll just have the coffee.'

'Sure?' He took a frying-pan out of the cupboard and set it on the old gas stove with a clatter that made her jump this time.

'Quite sure,' she said firmly, trying to inject some resolve into her voice in the hope that it would convince her as well as him that she knew what she wanted.

Did she? an insidious little voice suddenly whispered inside her head. Was she one hundred per cent certain that she wouldn't regret this? All she had to do was tell him that she'd changed her mind and...

What? Go back to the status quo, to a life spent hundreds of miles apart from her husband? Was that what she really wanted, to carry on the way they had been doing?

She knew the answer to that question, knew,

too, that divorce was their only option now. Seb would be better off without her and she most certainly would be happier if she wasn't living in a state of perpetual limbo!

Seb finished frying the bacon then poured them both a mug of coffee. Libby thanked him politely when he put the mug in front of her.

'No problem,' he assured her, going back to fetch the milk out of the fridge. He added a splash to her mug then went back again to assemble his sandwich. It seemed to take for ever before he had it done to his satisfaction, and by that time her nerves were in shreds. As soon as he sat down, she got straight to the point.

'Look, Seb, I can't see any point in dragging this out. You know why I'm here so let's sort things out and then I can leave you in peace.' She shrugged, wishing she felt anywhere near as calm as she was pretending to be. 'We're both adults and we both know the score. I can't see that we need to fight about this, do you?'

'I have no intention of fighting with you, Libby.' He put his sandwich back on the plate and looked at her. 'I don't want to make this any more difficult for you than it already is.'

'Thank you. I…I appreciate that.' She forced down the lump that had risen to her throat because she couldn't afford to let her emotions get the better of her. 'I suppose the main thing we need to decide is what we should do with the house in Sussex and all our belongings. I'm willing to buy you out, if you'll let me, but there's all the other things like furniture, for instance. Half of it is yours so we need to decide who keeps what.'

'You can have it all.'

Seb picked up his sandwich but the bread tasted like sawdust once it was in his mouth. Maybe he did want Libby to be happy but he wasn't sure if he could behave in a civilised fashion while they dotted all the Is and crossed the Ts. He didn't give a damn what happened to the bloody furniture or the house! It was Libby he cared about, Libby and the fact that she might be leaving him for someone else.

Pain sliced through him once more. The thought of her sharing her life with anyone except him was more than he could bear. It wouldn't be *his* arms she fell asleep in each night, and it wouldn't be *him* she woke up next to each morning. Some other guy would lie beside her and make plans for their future together.

They were bound to have a family, of course. Libby had always wanted children and she wouldn't want to waste too much time making her dream come true. The thought of her being pregnant with another man's child made him want to throw up, even though he had no right to feel that way.

He'd had his chance and wasted it. He'd wanted his dream job as well as her, but he'd been too greedy, hadn't he? He should have realised that he could have one or the other, not both. If he could turn back the clock, he would have refused the job and concentrated on his marriage, but it wasn't going to happen. All those wasted hours had melted away and he wouldn't get them back again. He was going to lose her and there wasn't a damned thing he could do to stop it happening!

'Oh, no. That wouldn't be right. It's only

fair that you should have half of everything. I mean, some of the things must have sentimental value…'

'I've already told you that I don't want anything. You can keep the lot. It's up to you what you do with it.'

He picked up his plate and went over to the waste bin. Libby frowned as she watched him toss the sandwich into the bin. It just didn't seem fair that he should hand over everything to her…

Unless he didn't want any mementoes of their life together?

Pain rushed through her and she stood up abruptly, devastated by how that thought made her feel. That Seb should want to erase her from his life hurt unbearably yet what had she expected him to do? He had made a new life for himself here so why would he want anything that reminded him of their time together?

'If that's what you want, it's fine by me. If you change your mind, just tell me.'

'I won't.' He put the plate on the counter and turned to face her. 'So is that it, then? There's nothing else that needs sorting out?'

'Not that I can think of. I imagine the next step is to find ourselves a solicitor.'

'I'll use the firm that handled the conveyancing when I bought this house. I have their address somewhere about so I'll text you with the details.'

'Thanks. I'll pass them on to my solicitor.' She picked up her bag and shrugged. 'That seems to be it. There isn't much more we can do until the divorce papers are prepared.'

'It shouldn't take long to finalise things,' he assured her emotionlessly. 'Marilyn's divorce came through earlier on in the year and she told me that it had taken just a few months. Apparently, it's quite a simple process if neither party contests it.'

'Good. The sooner the better, as far as I'm concerned.'

She turned away before he could see how wounded she felt. It was obvious that he couldn't wait to be rid of her.

'That sounds as though you've been making plans for the future,' he observed, following her into the hall.

'Do you blame me?' she countered, doing

her best to disguise her devastation. She wasn't naïve enough to imagine that Seb would be on his own for very long after they split up.

'No, I don't blame you at all. You deserve to be happy, Libby.'

His voice grated and she paused when she heard the strain it held. 'So do you, Seb. Just because we're getting divorced, it doesn't mean that I don't care about you. I…I hope that you will be happy, too.'

'Thank you.'

He walked past her and opened the front door, making it clear that he didn't want to linger over their goodbyes. Libby quickly followed him because she didn't want to linger either, yet as she reached the step she could feel tears welling to her eyes. This would be the last time she saw him. She certainly wouldn't make the journey up here again, and Seb most definitely wouldn't drive all the way to Sussex when there was no reason to do so. This was, in effect, the end of their marriage.

'Please, don't cry, Libby. It's what you wanted, isn't it? So there's no reason to upset yourself.'

'It's just so sad,' she whispered, choking back a sob.

'It is.' He pulled her into his arms and held her tightly against him, his lips brushing her hair so that if she hadn't known better she might have believed that everything was going to be fine. But it wouldn't be fine because they were breaking up. Quite frankly, she didn't know how she was going to live without him!

'Seb…' she began desperately, as panic gripped her, but he shook his head.

'No. There's no point saying anything else. We just have to accept what's happened and think about the future now.'

He kissed her lightly on her forehead then stepped back, and there was something so final about the gesture that she knew it would be pointless to argue. 'Goodbye, Libby. Take care of yourself.'

'You, too,' she whispered.

She turned and ran to her car, not looking back as she started the engine. There was nothing to look back for because this was the end: the end of her marriage, the end of Seb loving her.

Tears streamed down her face and she had to stop when she reached the road because she couldn't see where she was going. The pearly morning light had faded to a bleak greyness now which mirrored her mood. Her whole future felt grey and bleak now that Seb wouldn't play any part in it.

Fear gripped her again and just for a moment she wondered if she should go back and tell him that she'd changed her mind. Then sanity returned. Why would he want her to go back when he'd just let her go?

She dried her eyes then set off, following the route they'd taken on their way to the house. And each mile she drove was one mile further away from Seb and one mile closer to that lonely future she couldn't bear to imagine.

CHAPTER TWENTY

Saturday: 10 a.m.

SEB sat at the kitchen table, uncaring that the cup of coffee he had poured for himself was growing cold. *Libby had left him and their marriage was over.*

The words hammered inside his skull, over and over again, but he still couldn't believe it had actually happened. Closing his eyes, he tried to make sense of what had gone on, but that only made matters worse. All he could picture was the expression on her face as she'd walked out of the door…

Pain ripped through him and he opened his eyes and stared around the empty room. It summed up what his life was going to be like in the future: empty, cold, bleak. Without

Libby, he'd lost his centre, his reason for being. Oh, he would go through the motions, of course, but nothing he achieved from this point on would afford him any real pleasure.

Pushing back his chair, he stood up, feeling weariness dragging at him. He desperately needed to sleep but he was far too keyed up to go to bed. He went into the sitting room instead and sat down on the sofa, trying not to think about the plans he'd made when he had bought the house. There was no point imagining how cosy this room would have looked once Libby had worked her magic on it because it wasn't going to happen. She would be too busy creating a new home for herself and his successor!

Seb swore colourfully, pain and anger finding an outlet in the ugly words. He didn't feel any better after the outburst was over but he didn't feel any worse either. Resting his head against the cushions, he tried to doze but his mind wouldn't allow him to rest. If it wouldn't have elicited a lot of curious comments, he would have gone back to work, but the last thing he needed was people asking him what was wrong. He had to stay here and pray that he would find a way to cope.

Eventually.

Libby spotted a sign for the motorway as soon as she reached the town centre. She followed the directions and eventually arrived at the junction.

She headed south, trying not to think about what had happened between her and Seb. She'd achieved what she had set out to do yesterday and now she must concentrate on the future. Although she enjoyed general practice work, she wasn't sure if she wanted to remain in her present post. Maybe it was time to move on and opt for a partnership this time? She'd always liked the idea of working in a small rural practice so that's what she would aim for. Her parents had retired to Portugal a few years ago so it wasn't as though she had ties to any particular part of the country. She could remain down south or move further north—where Seb lived was a beautiful area and she could imagine herself living by the coast…

She caught herself up short when she realised how improbable that scenario was and concentrated on her driving. The traffic was quite heavy now and there were a lot of lorries in the inside lane, which were slowing things down. She was just about to pull out and overtake the car in front of her when it suddenly shot into the middle lane at the same moment as a car in the outside lane pulled in.

Libby gasped in horror as the two vehicles collided. She stamped on her brakes and just managed to avoid a collision when one of the vehicles shot across in front of her and careered up the banking at the side of the carriageway. She had no idea what had happened to the other car, she was too busy trying to get out of the way. But as soon as she judged it safe to do so, she pulled up on the hard shoulder and got out of her car.

The traffic had come to a standstill and she could see a number of vehicles strewn across the carriageway. Snatching her bag out of the boot, she ran back along the hard shoulder and scrambled up the banking to where the first car was precariously balanced on its roof. The driver—a young woman—was hanging upside down from her seat belt and Libby realised that she would need help to get her out. Fortunately there were a couple of men already there so once she'd explained that she was a doctor, she enlisted their help.

The door was jammed shut but one of the men had a crowbar and managed to force it open. Libby knelt down beside the car and spoke to the girl. 'Can you tell me where it hurts?'

'My neck…and my legs…' The girl tried to wriggle free of the harness but Libby stopped her.

'I want you to keep very still. We're going to get you out of there but we need to make sure that your neck is supported first so I'm going to put a collar on you.'

The girl began to cry. 'My dad's going to kill me when he sees what I've done to his car. I only passed my test last week and he made me promise that I wouldn't go on the motorway until I'd had a bit more practice.'

Libby sighed softly. 'I'm sure he'll be more relieved that you're all right than angry. My name's Libby, by the way, and I'm a doctor. What's your name?'

'Amy.'

'Right, then, Amy, let's get that collar on you then we can see if we can get you out of there.'

It was a bit of struggle to fix the collar from that position, but she managed it in the end. Releasing the harness proved to be even more difficult because the buckle had jammed. Fortunately, the police arrived very quickly and they had a special device to cut through the webbing strap.

'Be very careful with her,' she instructed as the men lifted the girl out of the car. 'Try not to jolt her spine.'

They laid her on the grass so that Libby could examine her. Both femurs were broken and the bone was protruding through the flesh of the left leg. She covered the open wound with a sterile dressing to protect it then examined the girl's spine—sliding her hand beneath Amy's back to check the alignment of the vertebrae. She breathed a sigh of relief when she didn't detect any obvious abnormalities, although it didn't prove conclusively that there was no damage. Amy would need to be X-rayed before they could be certain about that.

The ambulances had started to arrive so she relayed her findings to the paramedics and handed the girl over to them. A lot of people had been injured, although there were no fatalities, thankfully enough. Even the driver of the second car involved in the collision had received only minor injuries.

It could have been a lot worse, she thought as she watched the paramedics load Amy on board the ambulance. Nobody knew what was going to happen to them in the future, which made it all the more important to live life to the full while you had the chance. She should have done that this past year. She should have gone with Seb and made sure they lived every second as though it were their last. Now it was too late for them and the thought was just too much to bear.

Sitting down on the banking, she cried as all

the pain and heartache caught up with her. Her marriage was over and she had lost Seb for good.

It was no good. He couldn't sit here and try to sleep when his life was in tatters. He had to do something to sort it out!

Seb leapt to his feet, desperately wishing that he hadn't let Libby leave like that. He should have kept her here and done everything he could to make her understand how much he loved her. He refused to accept that she didn't feel anything for him any more. If only he'd explained that he couldn't face the thought of living without her then she might have reconsidered and given him another chance. But instead of doing that, he'd led her to believe that he no longer cared. Hell and damnation. What had he done?

He strode out of the room, pausing only long enough to snatch up his car keys. Maybe he wouldn't be able to persuade her to come back to him but he had to try. He couldn't bear to be left wondering if there'd been something more he could have done to save their marriage so he would go after her and beg her to listen to him. There had to be a way to convince her that this divorce shouldn't go ahead!

He ran out to his car and started the engine. He knew that she would head for the motorway and with a bit of luck he might be able to catch up with her before she reached it. However, he was quite prepared to drive all the way to Sussex if need be, and the thought made him groan out loud in despair.

If only he'd realised sooner how important it was to keep their marriage alive, he would have driven down to see her every single weekend. And when he'd got there, he wouldn't have left her in any doubt about his feelings either. He loved her, he wanted her and he should have told her that instead of letting his stupid pride get in the way.

Seb's mouth thinned. No matter what else transpired that day, he intended to tell Libby that he loved her. It was the least he could do after all the heartache he'd caused her this past year.

Seb could feel his anxiety mounting as he joined the motorway. Although he'd made ex-

cellent time, there'd been no sign of Libby and
he couldn't pretend that he wasn't worried
about her. She'd always been a careful driver
but he knew how upset she'd been when she'd
left the house. The thought of her having an
accident was more than he could bear. If any
harm came to her because of him, he wouldn't
be able to live with himself!

The thought had barely crossed his mind
when he heard sirens. Glancing in his rear-view
mirror, he saw a convoy of ambulances
speeding down the outside lane. The traffic hurriedly moved out of the way to let them pass,
and Seb didn't hesitate. He slipped into the gap
behind them, feeling his heart thundering as he
followed them down the motorway. There'd obviously been an accident and all he could do
now was pray that Libby hadn't been involved
in it.

The traffic had come to a standstill now but
he had no difficulty getting through as part of
the convoy. They reached the site where the
accident had happened and his heart turned
over when he saw all the vehicles scattered

across the carriageway. There seemed to be dozens of cars with dents in them, although he couldn't see Libby's car anywhere about, thankfully. He breathed a sigh of relief as he pulled up on the hard shoulder. At least she was safe so now he would see if there was anything he could to help the other people.

He took his case out of the boot and ran towards the nearest vehicle, a van. There were two men in it and they both looked dazed. One of them had a cut over his right eye, which was pouring with blood, so Seb gave him a wad of lint and told him to apply pressure to it. The other man shook his head when Seb asked him if he was hurt so he moved on to the next vehicle. The driver, a woman in her twenties, was moaning softly and his heart sank when he realised that she was pregnant.

'How many weeks are you?' he asked, crouching down beside the car.

'Thirty-eight,' she whispered. She clutched her stomach and groaned. 'I've got these awful pains…'

She broke off, sweat beading on her upper lip

as the pain intensified. Seb guessed that she had gone into labour and if that was the case then he needed to get her out of the car. Reaching over, he unfastened her seat belt.

'We need to get you out of there. Do you think you can walk if I help you?'

'I think so…' She swung her feet out of the footwell then had to stop as another contraction began. As soon as it had passed, he helped her to the hard shoulder. The paramedics were busy tending the rest of the injured so he spread his jumper on the ground and sat her down.

'I'm going to fetch a blanket,' he explained when she looked at him in alarm. 'I won't be long so just stay there and I'll be right back.'

He ran over to the nearest ambulance and explained what was happening. One of the crew gave him a blanket and assured him that he would come over to help as soon as he could.

Seb swung round to go back to the woman then stopped dead when he suddenly spotted Libby's car parked on the hard shoulder. He ran over to it but there was no sign of her inside.

Panic gripped him as he turned and stared at the scene of chaos around him.

Where was she?

CHAPTER TWENTY-ONE

Saturday: 11 a.m.

'SEB! What are you *doing* here?'

Libby could scarcely believe her own eyes when she spotted Seb standing beside her car. He turned when he heard her calling him and her heart leapt when she saw the expression on his face. She didn't think she'd ever seen anyone who'd looked more desperate.

'Libby!' He ran towards her and unceremoniously hauled her into his arms. 'Thank God, you're all right. I was terrified that something had happened to you when I saw your car.'

'I'm fine. It was the car in front of me that was involved in the collision…' She broke off and shuddered as she realised how close she'd come to being injured.

'It's all right, darling. It's all over now and I won't let anything happen to you—I swear.'

He pulled her closer and held her as though he would never let her go again. Libby closed her eyes as a feeling of relief swept over her. Everything would be all right now that Seb was with her. He had been her protector and her lover for such a long time that she simply couldn't imagine being without him and didn't want to try. Maybe it was stupid even to think of trying to mend their marriage after she'd told him that she wanted a divorce, but she couldn't just let him go. She needed him too much, wanted him, loved him, and that had to count for something, didn't it?

Tipping back her head, she looked into his eyes. 'I wouldn't have been so frightened if you'd been with me. I know it's probably too late to ask you this but do you think we could try again to make our marriage work? I don't want to lose you, Seb. Really, I don't.'

'I… You… Oh, hell, I can't seem to think straight, let alone speak!'

Libby gasped as he bent and kissed her with a

hunger that answered her question far better than any words could have done. When he drew back, she clung to him, not wanting to let him go again.

'I love you, Libby. I don't want a divorce either. I never have done. I want to spend the rest of my life with you—if you'll let me?'

Tears misted her eyes when she heard the uncertainty in his voice. It was all her fault that he should wonder if she loved him, and it was up to her to convince him that she did.

'I don't want a divorce either. I only suggested it because I was so desperate. I've missed you so much, Seb, and I don't want us to carry on living apart the way we've been doing. I want to be with you every single day of my life.'

'It's what I want, too,' he said simply. He kissed her again, softly and with a wealth of promise, and she shivered. It felt as though a whole new chapter in their life had begun. The future was no longer bleak but filled with light and colour now that Seb would be there to share it with her.

'I love you,' she told him, not wanting there to be any mistake about her feelings either.

'And I love you, too.' He lifted her hand to his mouth and kissed her palm with a tenderness that made the tears flow down her cheeks when she realised what could have happened if he hadn't come after her. She could have lost him for good and it would have been her own fault, too.

'Don't. We've both made mistakes, me more than you. I should never have left you behind and moved so far away. It was bound to have had an effect on our marriage and I shall always blame myself for that.'

'And I shouldn't have let you go,' she said honestly, because it wasn't fair to let him shoulder all the blame. She would have said more but just then he gasped.

'Heavens, I almost forgot that poor woman!'

'Which woman?' Libby demanded as he grabbed hold of her hand.

'She was in one of the cars near the back of the pile-up. She's thirty-eight weeks pregnant and it looks as if she's gone into labour. One of the paramedics offered to keep an eye on her but I need to get back and see what's happening.'

'Oh, the poor thing!' Libby exclaimed, hurrying after him. She ran forward when she saw the woman sitting on the ground and knelt down beside her. 'Hi, I'm Libby and I'm a doctor,' she told her, seeing the relief that crossed the woman's face. She turned to the paramedic, 'How far apart are the contractions?'

'Just a few minutes now—they seem to have speeded up.'

Just then another contraction began. Seb knelt down and spread the blanket over the woman.

'This will help to keep her warm as well as afford her a bit of privacy,' he told Libby quietly. He waited until the pain had passed then smiled at the woman. 'Is it OK if I take a look to see how things are progressing? My name's Seb, by the way, and I'm a doctor, too. I've delivered my share of babies over the years, although I have to confess that I've not delivered one at the side of the road before!'

'I'm Sarah…Sarah Hartwell.' The woman smiled at him. 'And I wasn't planning on giving birth here, if it's any consolation. I had a birth plan all worked out with my midwife but I can't see that happening now, can you?'

Libby laughed. 'Some things are just not meant to be. So long as your baby is safe, that's all that matters.'

'He will be all right, won't he?' Sarah asked anxiously.

'He should be fine,' Seb assured her. 'Now, you just concentrate on your breathing while we help that little chap out of there.'

Libby gripped the young woman's hand as another contraction began. Seb quickly removed her underclothes and examined her. 'Baby's head is crowning,' he told Libby quietly. 'It won't be long now, from the look of things.'

In the end it was a textbook delivery. Just ten minutes later, Sarah had a healthy baby boy in her arms. Libby sighed with pleasure as she looked at him.

'He is just so gorgeous!'

'Isn't he just?' Sarah pressed a gentle kiss on her son's cheek then smiled at them. 'Thank you so much for helping me. I don't know what I would have done if you all hadn't been here.'

'It was our pleasure.' Seb grinned then put his arm around Libby's shoulders and kissed her on the cheek. Sarah smiled as she looked at them.

'I take it that you two haven't just met, then?'

'No. We've been married for over eight years and we intend to stay married for the rest of our lives,' Seb said firmly, glancing at Libby with an expression in his eyes that turned her knees to water.

They handed Sarah and her baby over to the paramedics and had just waved her off when a police officer came over to speak to them.

'We're taking the names and addresses of everyone who was involved in the incident,' he informed them. 'We need to speak to you at a later date so if you could let me have phone numbers as well, it would be a big help.'

Libby gave him her address then glanced at Seb and smiled. 'I'd better give you my mobile phone number just in case you need to contact me. I might not get back to Sussex for a few days.'

She wrote down her mobile phone number and gave it to him. Seb didn't say a word the whole time she was doing it, but she knew that he had realised the significance of what she'd done. As soon as the policeman left, he led her to his car and helped her inside. Libby smiled at him when he got in beside her.

'You do have room for a guest, I hope? I thought I would stay with you, if you'll have me, of course.'

'Oh, I'll have you all right.' Leaning over he dropped a kiss on her mouth. 'I love you, Dr Bridges.'

'I love you, too, Dr Bridges.' She cupped his cheek, savouring the moment because just a short time before she'd never believed it would happen. It was like having all her dreams come true...well, almost all.

She smiled up at him, not even attempting to hide how much she wanted him. 'Why don't you drive us both home so I can show you just how much?'

CHAPTER TWENTY-TWO

Saturday: 12 p.m.

PALE winter sunlight streamed through the bedroom window and Libby sighed with pleasure. They had left her car at the motorway service station and driven back to the house in Seb's. Neither of them had said much on the journey—it hadn't been necessary. It had been enough to know that they were back together, although they would have to talk everything through at some point.

'You must be tired.' Seb came up behind her and enfolded her in his arms. Libby smiled as she nestled back against him, loving the feel of his strong body pressed against hers.

'Not *that* tired.'

'Does that mean what I think it does?' he

murmured, his lips nuzzling the hollow behind her right ear.

'There's an easy way to find out,' she replied saucily, tilting her head to the side to give him easier access.

She shivered when she felt his lips skate down her neck and across her nape. She had always enjoyed the physical side of their relationship and had missed making love with him this past year.

'I want to kiss you, too,' she protested, trying to turn around, but he wouldn't let her move.

'In a minute. You have no idea how often I've dreamed of this moment, sweetheart. I've lain awake many a night, imagining how it would feel to make love to you right here with that view spread out in front of us.'

He kissed her again, his hands moving round her body to cup her breasts. 'It will be like touching heaven. And we will do it together.'

Libby shivered when she heard the passion in his voice. That Seb still wanted her this much made a mockery of her fears about there being someone else in his life. It was her he wanted and only her, and knowing that made her feel like the luckiest woman alive.

She closed her eyes as he stroked and caressed her. She was still wearing the shirt she'd worn yesterday and a bra but he soon dispensed with them. She could feel the heat building deep inside as he gently teased her nipples until they peaked. She almost begged him to stop at that point because it was the sweetest kind of torment to have him caress her and not be able to reciprocate. But then his hand moved lower, sliding inside the waistband of her trousers so that he could stroke her stomach, and her protest quickly changed to words of encouragement.

'Let's not rush things.' Seb brushed her cheek with his lips, his hands stilling as he drew her back against him so that she could feel the hardness of his erection pressing against her. 'We have all the time in the world to enjoy each other so let's make this a truly special time for us both.'

Libby didn't argue, although she wasn't sure if she could hold on for very much longer. Each touch, each caress, each kiss was building up to a crescendo of sensation that she wasn't sure she could control. She put her arms down at her sides and kept them there as his fingers skated ever closer to the very heart of her femininity. It was only when she felt him touch the source of all the heat that she couldn't hold out any longer.

She turned to face him, not attempting to hide how aroused she felt because there was no need. Seb wanted her just as much as she wanted him. He rained kisses over her face and breasts then looked deep into her eyes.

'I love you, Libby. No matter what mistakes I've made in the past year, I never stopped loving you.'

'I love you, too…so much,' she whispered, aching for him to consummate their love.

He must have understood how desperate she was because his hands were urgent as he peeled away the rest of her clothes. Libby helped him, wanting only to be free of any restraints which might hinder their love-making. Once she was naked, he stripped off his own clothes and lifted her into his arms, entering her with one long powerful thrust which made her cry out his name.

Libby clung to him as passion swept them both away. She could feel the coldness of the wall against her back and the contrast between that and the fierce heat of Seb's body made her shudder. When she was close to him she would always be warm. It was only when they were apart that she felt chilled to her soul, but they would never be apart again. They both climaxed together and it just seemed to put the seal on their new-found happiness. They were meant to be together and nothing would separate them ever again.

Seb knew that their love-making had reached new heights that day. As he carried Libby to the bed and laid her down, he was filled with awe. They *had* glimpsed heaven just now in one another's arms, and it seemed to prove that their love for one another was something really special.

There were tears in his eyes when she pulled him down to lie beside her. 'Don't ever let me go again, Seb, will you?'

'I won't.' He kissed her softly on the mouth

then stroked her cheek, wanting to soothe any lingering fears she might have. 'I meant every one of my marriage vows, my darling, and I won't ever break them.'

'I won't either,' she whispered, snuggling against him as exhaustion took its toll on her.

Seb pulled the quilt over them and cradled her, overwhelmed by the wonder of what had happened. That he had won back the right to hold her like this seemed almost too much. He didn't deserve such happiness after the way he'd let her down but he swore on his life that he would do everything he could to make up for it.

'Go to sleep,' he murmured, his voice thickened with emotion. He kissed the top of her head, hoping she knew how precious she was to him. 'I'll be here when you wake up.'

'Promise?' she said sleepily, and he laughed tenderly.

'I don't need to promise. There's nowhere I would rather be than right here with you in this bed, believe me.'

She relaxed against him and some of the knots in his heart slowly unravelled. She trusted him to keep his word and it was more than he had dared hope for at one point. No matter what happened in the future, he would never let her down again. He would never let her leave him either. He needed her and she needed him—they would be together for ever.

A feeling of euphoria filled him as he settled back against the pillows. His marriage had survived and he had his wife back in his arms. The future had never looked brighter!

CHAPTER TWENTY-THREE

Saturday: 1 p.m.

'I CAN'T believe I fell asleep!' Libby dragged herself up against the pillows. She frowned when Seb laughed. 'What's so funny?'

'You are.' He kissed the tip of her nose and grinned at her. 'You were up all last night so it's hardly surprising that you nodded off for a few minutes, is it?'

'Maybe not,' she conceded. 'But you were awake all last night, too, and you didn't fall asleep.'

'No. But that's because I was too busy watching you. Have I ever told you how beautiful you look when you're sleeping, Mrs Bridges?'

'No, but don't let that deter you from telling

me now.' She snuggled up against him. 'Are you sure I don't snore or sleep with my mouth open?'

'It wouldn't matter even if you did. You would still look sexy and adorable and I'd still love you.' He planted a kiss on the tip of her nose, loving the feeling of closeness that came from being able to tease her like this. 'I'm totally smitten. I'd probably still feel the same even if you drooled all over your pillow!'

'I shall remind you of that when I'm old and grey and all my teeth have fallen out,' she retorted, laughing.

'So long as you intend to be old, grey and toothless with me then it's a deal.' He kissed her again, on the mouth this time, and felt his body immediately stir to life. 'Sorry!' he murmured, pulling away. 'I'm not trying to be a glutton—honest. It's just that it's been such a long time since we were together like this.'

'It is. And it won't happen again.' She tipped back her head to look at him and he could see a trace of uncertainty in her eyes. 'I want to be with you from now on, Seb, but I'll understand if it's not possible to do that immediately.'

'Not possible?' he repeated, unsure what she meant by that.

'I mean that if you've been seeing someone else, obviously you will have to sort things out—'

'Hang on a second! What do you mean—*if* I've been seeing someone else?' He propped himself up on his elbow and glowered at her. 'There has never been anyone but you, Libby, from the moment we met. I thought you knew that?'

'I did…but last night I started wondering if you'd met someone else since you'd moved up here…' She broke off and swallowed. 'I was wrong, wasn't I?'

'Yes, you were,' he said firmly. 'I'm not interested in anyone else. The only woman in my life is you. I don't know where you got the idea that I was seeing someone, but it isn't true.' He shrugged. 'Most of the time I've lived up here, I've been working, not socialising. What free time I've had has been spent house-hunting. There is no other woman, Libby. There never will be either because no other woman could compare to you.'

'I feel exactly the same,' she admitted, blinking away her tears. 'I've never wanted anyone but you, Seb.'

He pulled her into his arms, wondering if he should confess that he'd also had his doubts. He didn't want anything to spoil their reunion but deep down he knew that he had to tell her the truth. Their marriage had been founded on honesty and he didn't want anything to change.

'I wondered if you'd maybe found someone else as well,' he admitted roughly, because the thought still hurt. He felt her stiffen and hurried on. 'I'm sorry I doubted you, Libby, but I couldn't see why you would want to stay with me when I'd let you down so badly.'

'You didn't let me down. What happened was the very natural result of the way we were living. We were both working so hard that we had very little time for ourselves.'

'But if I hadn't been so bloody selfish and accepted this job then none of this would have happened.'

'Oh, I think it could have done. At some point we would have reached a crisis point and it just so happened that it coincided with you ac-cepting the job up here.' She kissed him gently on the mouth. 'Don't beat yourself up, Seb. It happened and we got through it. Our marriage will be stronger than ever now because we both know how close we came to losing each other.'

'I will never do anything to put our relation-ship at risk again.' He kissed her hard, wanting her to believe him, and she sighed.

'Neither will I, which is why I intend to hand in my notice and move up here just as soon as I can arrange it.'

'No! It's not fair that you should have to give up your job.'

'I'm not doing it because I have to.' She placed a finger on his lips. 'I'm doing it because I want to. I want to be with you and I most definitely want to wake up each morning to that view. It's fabulous!'

'Oh, I see.' Seb chuckled. 'You'll make me jealous if that's the only thing you want to wake up for.'

'Oh, there might be other advantages to living here,' she conceded. She turned into his arms and batted her eyelashes at him. 'Want to help me make a list, my darling husband?'

'Of course.' He pulled her to him and smiled into her eyes, knowing that he was the luckiest man alive. 'After all, it's a husband's duty to take proper care of his wife.'

Libby didn't argue about that. She obviously agreed with him.

CHAPTER TWENTY-FOUR

Saturday: 2 p.m.

'THANKS for letting me know… Yes, Libby's right here so I'll tell her.'

Seb hung up the phone and made his way to the kitchen, where Libby was in the process of making them a meal. She looked round when she heard him coming in and smiled.

'I take it that was work?'

'How did you guess?' He went over and kissed her, grinning when she playfully pushed him away.

'I'm supposed to be making you something to eat like a dutiful little wife!'

Seb snorted. 'You're not the dutiful type!'

'Is that a fact?' She pulled a face at him as she

cracked open an egg and slid it into the hot fat. 'I hope that wasn't a complaint?'

'No way! I like you just the way you are and I don't ever want you to change.'

'That's all right, then.' She wiped her hands on a teatowel then turned to him. 'So what's happened now?'

'Apparently, the tanker's owners have admitted that they didn't have a licence to transport those chemicals. It turns out that there's a ban on them being imported into the country.'

'Really? No wonder they were so reluctant to tell the coastguard anything.'

'It does help to explain it. Anyway, the relevant authorities are going to get in touch with the firm that placed the order and I imagine they will be in a lot of trouble.'

'What will happen about the chemicals, though? Will they be returned to their point of origin?'

'That's the tricky bit.' He sighed. 'It turns out that the tanker hadn't been passed as seaworthy before it set sail so there's no way they can send it back to its home port.'

'Why on earth did the captain agree to the trip in that case?' she exclaimed. 'I mean, he had his wife and his son on board with him so why would he take such a risk?'

'Sheer desperation, I expect. He's told the authorities that he was threatened with the sack if he refused to sail. If that had happened, he'd have had no means to support his family. Apparently, everyone in his home town works for the same chemical manufacturing company. There's no other work available.'

'Which is probably why most of those men were on that tanker. They must have known about the risks it involved but there was nothing they could do about it.' She shook her head. 'I wonder if the chemicals have leaked before?'

'Oh, I'd say so, which means that most of the men will have been exposed to the dangers over a prolonged period of time.'

'No wonder that seaman went missing from the hospital,' she said sadly. 'Anything would be better than the kind of life he must have been leading—even being on the run.'

'It would. Apparently, some of the men—in-

cluding the captain and his family—have said
that they intend to apply for permission to stay
in this country.'

'Do you think they will be allowed to do so?'

'I don't know, to be honest. But it certainly
sounds as though they would have a good
reason to back up their applications.' He
frowned. 'Maybe we can do something to help
them—set up an appeal or something. I'd hate
to think of them being sent back to a place like
that to live, wouldn't you?'

'Yes, I would.' She scooped the egg out of the
pan and popped it on a plate then smiled at him.
'It makes you realise how lucky we are, doesn't
it?'

'It does.' He took the spatula out of her hand
and turned off the gas then pulled her to him.
'And we're luckier than anyone else because
we have each other. I don't think I would want
to carry on without you, Libby. You are my
whole world.'

'And you're mine.' She kissed him tenderly.
'I can think of just one thing that would make
our lives even better.'

'A family.' He cupped her face in his hands. 'It would be the icing on the cake, wouldn't it, sweetheart?'

'It would.' She kissed him again then whirled out of his arms and ran to the door.

'Where are you going? I thought we were having something to eat.'

'That can wait' She held out her hand. 'We have a baby to make, Seb. Are you coming?'

'Just you try and stop me!'

MEDICAL ROMANCE™

Large Print

Titles for the next six months…

MILLS & BOON®

0407 LP 2P P1 Medic

MEDICAL ROMANCE™

Large Print

August

A WIFE AND CHILD TO CHERISH   Caroline Anderson
THE SURGEON'S FAMILY MIRACLE   Marion Lennox
A FAMILY TO COME HOME TO   Josie Metcalfe
THE LONDON CONSULTANT'S RESCUE   Joanna Neil
THE DOCTOR'S BABY SURPRISE   Gill Sanderson
THE SPANISH DOCTOR'S CONVENIENT BRIDE
Meredith Webber

September

A FATHER BEYOND COMPARE   Alison Roberts
AN UNEXPECTED PROPOSAL   Amy Andrews
SHEIKH SURGEON, SURPRISE BRIDE   Josie Metcalfe
THE SURGEON'S CHOSEN WIFE   Fiona Lowe
A DOCTOR WORTH WAITING FOR   Margaret McDonagh
HER L.A. KNIGHT   Lynne Marshall

October

HIS VERY OWN WIFE AND CHILD   Caroline Anderson
THE CONSULTANT'S NEW-FOUND FAMILY   Kate Hardy
CITY DOCTOR, COUNTRY BRIDE   Abigail Gordon
THE EMERGENCY DOCTOR'S DAUGHTER   Lucy Clark
A CHILD TO CARE FOR   Dianne Drake
HIS PREGNANT NURSE   Laura Iding

MILLS & BOON®

0407 LP 2P P2 Medical